THE PERFECT PAINKILLER

So far, things hadn't been working out so well for Skye Fargo. His head was aching from a beating two Comanches had given him. His chest was still bleeding under bandages from the cutting job that a beautiful, cold-blooded squaw had done on him.

But the girl named Jane was doing what she could.

She was pressing against him. Her breath was warm on his neck. And she grinned at him with a wicked little twist to her mouth as she moved even closer—with deliberate intent.

"I always heard that it takes a man's mind off his hurts," she said.

"Does it really work?" said Fargo.

Jane began to wriggle. Very slowly but very insistently.

"I think it's working," the Trailsman said. . . .

THE TRAILSMAN 62

HORSETHIEF CROSSING

by

Jon Sharpe

A SIGNET BOOK

NEW AMERICAN LIBRARY

PUBLISHER'S NOTE

This novel is a work of fiction. Names, characters, places, and incidents either are the product of the author's imagination or are used fictitiously, and any resemblance to actual persons, living or dead, events, or locales is entirely coincidental.

The first chapter of this book previously appeared in *Bullet Caravan*, the sixty-first volume in this series.

The Trailsman

Beginnings . . . they bend the tree and they mark the man. Skye Fargo was born when he was eighteen. Terror was his midwife, vengeance his first cry. Killing spawned Skye Fargo, ruthless, cold-blooded murder. Out of the acrid smoke of gunpowder still hanging in the air, he rose, cried out a promise never forgotten.

The Trailsman they began to call him all across the West: searcher, scout, hunter, the man who could see where others only looked, his skills for hire but not his soul, the man who lived each day to the fullest, yet trailed each tomorrow. Skye Fargo, the Trailsman, the seeker who could take the wildness of a land and the wanting of a woman and make them his own.

San Antonio, Texas
1861

J se

1

The girl winked at him as she closed the door and slowly, deliberately slid the bolt to lock the two of them away from the rest of the world. She smiled in anticipation of a long and languid afternoon. That was fair enough. Skye Fargo was damn sure looking forward to it too.

Beyond the small window the sun was bright and hard, its harsh glare softened by a ragged length of muslin tacked above it. The room was not much, poorly furnished and seldom cleaned.

The girl, however, was something else again. She was as fine as the room was poor. Her hair and eyes were dark and gleaming, the shine of youth and health on her long, loose, raven-black hair, a bright, happy sparkle of mischief and joy showing in her eyes. She wore a peasant blouse, a loose-fitting skirt of homespun, and her legs and feet were bare, but no external trappings could lessen her loveliness. She was young and pretty and found the entire world full of joy.

With another wink and a short peal of irrepressible laughter that exposed tiny white teeth set against a dusky, matte-satin complexion, she reached high, having to rise on her tiptoes to give Fargo a brief kiss. Then she quickly began to peel out of her clothes.

Fargo began just as quickly to pull off his shirt. He kicked his boots off and let them drop unheeded into a corner of the little room.

He was a handsome man, a full head taller than the girl and with the lean-hipped, broad-shouldered build of the born horseman. His hair was near as dark as hers, but his lake-blue eyes were not so merry. Even in this moment of anticipated pleasures, there was a measure of reserve about him. A caution born of far trails and constant dangers.

He set a short, blunt Sharps carbine into a corner and unbuckled his gun belt to hang the Colt on the bedpost before he slid his trousers down and stood naked before the girl.

It had taken her only moments to undress. She was even lovelier now than he had expected, her breasts not overlarge but standing firm and proud and dark-tipped. Her legs were nicely formed if a trifle short for the rest of her fine frame. Her belly was nearly flat, soft and smooth, and only very slightly convex. Her pubic hair was a thick, curly patch of promise.

She smiled again, and Fargo held his arms open. She ran forward into them, and he held her close, the heat of his erection trapped between their bodies. He kissed her, having to lift her so that her feet dangled inches off the floor in order to make that contact. She laughed and explored his mouth hungrily with her tongue and mobile lips. Her mouth was exceptionally soft and her breath clean and tasting faintly of mint.

Fargo reached low, sliding his hand down her hip in a slow caress, and turned her in his arms so that he could put a forearm behind her knees and lift her. With another laugh she locked her arms around his neck and began to kiss his throat.

He carried her the few steps to the bed and sat with her in his lap, his cock pressing against her buttocks.

She wriggled, deliberately exciting him all the further, and was pleased with what she could see in his eyes.

Fargo cupped her right breast in his hand. It was firm and elastic, her flesh flowing in his fingers like moist clay, delightfully warm and sweet clay. He bent and took her nipple into his mouth, rolling it on his tongue and eliciting a sigh of pleasure from her.

She shifted off his lap and lay beside him so that she could touch and stroke and fondle him. Fargo offered no objection.

He nipped lightly at her other nipple with his lips and, carefully, with his teeth, and she sighed again.

"Love me, Skye. Please love me now."

Love. She meant it too. For Margarita this was no commercial exchange. There was nothing tawdry or sordid about it. For this delightful girl it truly was a matter of loving, one that she enjoyed and was pleased to give.

She opened herself to his touch, and she was already moistly eager for him. Tiny pearls of dewy wetness beaded the curling hairs that surrounded her opening. He slid a finger into her, surprised at the resistance he encountered there. Certainly not of any reluctance but the tightness of youth and perhaps even of relative inexperience.

He covered her, and she wrapped him in her arms and her legs and opened herself wide to welcome and receive him.

He had been right. She was extraordinarily tight, trapping him deep inside her body and surrounding him with damp heat.

"Let me?" she whispered.

He nodded and held himself braced rigid above her . . . and rigid as well within her.

Margarita began to move her hips, raising and lowering herself slowly, impaling herself. She shivered and shuddered with the pleasure of it as alternately he filled her and then was withdrawn almost to the point of losing contact with her.

Fargo didn't move at all. Margarita was doing more than enough for both of them. Her breathing quickened, and so did her motion, until she was pumping her hips wildly beneath him. She bucked and plunged, arching her neck, full lips drawn back from her teeth and eyes unfocused. "Ah . . . ah . . . ah . . . ahhhh!"

Fargo could feel the gather and rise of his own pleasure deep in his groin, spreading, filling him. The intense sensation drawn from the most distant parts of his body and flowing together in one concentrated rush that poured out of his balls, swelled his shaft to overflowing, and burst out of his body and into hers.

He shuddered, stiffened, and only in that last wild, uncontrolled moment plunged forward, throwing his weight onto and into her. Margarita clutched at him fiercely, arms and legs alike clamping hard around him, pulling him to her, pulling him into her greedily as the last convulsive shudderings of her own release turned into the joy of sharing his release.

She sighed and went limp beneath him. Fargo kissed her gently and lay for a time on top of her, his lean body pillowed on her smaller, softer length, his satiated member limp and wet but still deep inside her. Her breathing slowed; after a moment he rolled off her, and Margarita nestled close against him, unwilling to give up the contact with this darkly handsome *norteamericano*.

Far below and half a world away—or so it seemed at that moment—a piano tinkled faintly and voices were raised in laughter.

Fargo had stopped in at the saloon only for a beer to cut the dust of travel. He had found something far finer than anything that could be created by man. He rolled his head on the pillow to look into the wide, happy eyes of the girl and bent just enough to kiss the tip of her nose. Her upper lip wrinkled and she sneezed.

"Was that. . . ? No, couldn't be. Let me try it again." He kissed her there again, and she sneezed again. Both of them laughed. He rolled onto his side and pulled her to him for a proper kiss this time. Her breasts were warm and firm against his chest. She had been thoroughly satisfied but certainly not satiated. His kiss aroused her again. He could feel it in the change in her breathing, the slight quickening of it, and in the way she rubbed her hands up and down the hard planes of his back.

"Again? Yes?" She sounded immeasurably pleased by the idea.

"Again. Yes," he confirmed.

"You want me to help you?"

Before he could answer, Margarita disentangled herself from his arms and shifted low so that the ends of her hair trailed lazily across his belly.

She took him into her mouth and began to bob her head slowly up and down.

Far, far away, somewhere out in the glare of the sunlight, there was a rattle of small explosions. Gunfire. Heavy pistols, Fargo judged. Not that he cared at the moment.

Margarita stopped what she was doing and looked toward the window with wide, frightened eyes.

She looked damn cute like that, Fargo thought, with the head of his pecker clamped, but for the moment forgotten, between those pretty lips.

The fear that he could see in her eyes, though, wasn't cute at all. He stroked the back of her head. "Are you all right?"

She shuddered and pulled away from him, sitting up on the bed and hugging her arms tight around herself.

"The guns, they . . . I have seen bad things, Skye. So many bad things. I am sorry."

"It's all right, honey. We aren't in any hurry." He smiled at her reassuringly. "Will it make you feel any better if I take a look? Make sure nothing's wrong?"

She nodded quickly. Too quickly. She looked nervous.

He kissed her and said, "It will be all right. I won't let anything or anyone hurt you. I promise."

As if to make him out a liar, there was another hard rattle of gunfire from the street below. It sounded closer this time. Margarita turned her face away from the window and squeezed her eyes shut. She was pale and trembling.

Fargo petted her again and went to the window. He raised the scrap of muslin and looked down to the street.

From where he now was he couldn't see what the excitement was all about, but the people down below could. They were looking off toward Fargo's left toward something. A few were running for shelter. Others stood rooted where they were, spectating with open mouths and uncomprehending blank looks.

More gunshots sounded from the left, and across the street a man wearing a necktie and sleeve garters rushed out onto the sidewalk with a brace of old, large-caliber horse pistols.

A group of hard-charging riders—five, six of them— dashed into view to the left of Fargo's window. The storekeeper across the way raised one of his pistols and fired at them, hitting no one. He dropped the single-shot weapon and shifted the other to his right hand for another shot. The riders were virtually beneath Fargo's window now.

The storekeeper took aim. Three of the men on horse-back turned their revolvers toward the man. They fired, and one bullet caught the man low in the stomach, buckling him forward. His finger squeezed involuntarily on the trigger of the huge pistol, and the weapon belched flame and lead.

The unaimed shot caught a horse in the side of the head, dropping the animal into the dust of the street and spilling its rider.

The other men on horseback saw and wheeled, sending a shower of bullets down the street. One of them rode over to the storekeeper and made sure of him by sending a final slug into the back of his skull.

"Bastards," Fargo muttered.

The man who was down was trapped, his left foot caught by the weight of the carcass. He kicked and struggled and finally pulled himself free, his foot coming out bare except for a tattered sock. His boot remained under the dead horse.

Fargo expected the others to pick him up and ride double for their getaway. Instead, when he tried to mount behind the saddle of the nearest rider, the mounted man pushed him away and snapped something that Fargo couldn't hear through the glass of the window.

The downed man nodded and looked wildly about. Then he ran wildly toward the best horse he could see.

"Oh, shit," Fargo snarled.

The son of a bitch was headed toward the black-and-white Ovaro tied in front of the saloon, directly beneath the window where Fargo stood watching.

"No," Fargo bellowed, knowing even as he said it that if the man could hear, it would have no effect.

Fargo dashed across the small room and grabbed his Colt. By the time he got back to the window, the son of a bitch had the reins of the Ovaro free from the hitch rail. He vaulted into Fargo's saddle, and the Ovaro balked and curvetted.

Fargo snatched the muslin away from the window and tried to pull the window open. The damn thing was stuck.

He was in no humor to take time wrestling with it. He smashed the glass with the barrel of the Colt and quickly knocked the sharp shards of clinging glass away.

The falling glass got the attention of the men down below. They looked up and one of them fired, his bullet thudding into the wall just to the right of the window frame and ripping through the thin wood to send a shower of splinters into the room.

Fargo fired. The bastard on the Ovaro flinched. Fargo wasn't sure, but he thought he had hit him. How hard was another question.

One of the other riders grabbed the reins of the fidgety pinto, and the six of them bolted once again toward the right.

Fargo took aim on the back of the rider who was leading the Ovaro. He sighted carefully between and just below the shoulder blades. If he could knock that one out of the saddle, the pinto might stop where it was rather than join the rush of horses.

"Please no!"

Fargo felt his arm being dragged down just as he applied pressure on the trigger, and his shot went low, spending itself harmlessly in the dirt behind the heels of the retreating horses but sending up a spray of small gravel that only served to speed them along.

One of the riders threw a snap shot over his shoulder in Fargo's general direction. Fargo had no idea where that one went.

Down the block to the left more guns were firing now. The riders bent low and raked their horses with their spurs.

"Dammit, woman, leave me be." Fargo shook himself free of Margarita's panicky clinging and shoved her rudely away.

He spun back to the window with the Colt raised.

He was too late.

The horsemen swept around a corner and out of sight, leaving only dust and confusion behind them.

"Damn," Fargo groaned.

He was pissed. The girl was cowering at his feet, arms wrapped around his bare calves, crying, grabbing at him for whatever comfort and security he might have been able to offer for her terror.

He could see her fear and he was sorry for that, but he had no time for her right now. He rushed toward the door, then remembered that he was bare-ass naked and had to grab up his clothing.

By the time he had his trousers on he realized the futility of it.

Those men were mounted. One of them on the finest horse Skye Fargo had ever seen, dammit: on Skye Fargo's own Ovaro. Dammit.

There was no way he was going to catch them on foot.

Hopeless, he went back to the window.

A hurriedly assembled posse went thundering past, raising dust and hell but probably apt to raise little in the way of results.

The damn-fool townsmen hadn't taken the time to prepare for a long chase. They rode in whatever clothing they happened to be wearing at the time, and he could see no provisions or bedrolls tied behind their cantles.

They would be back soon, he figured, and empty-handed.

"Oh, hell," Fargo mumbled. He sat on the edge of the bed and took his time about getting his boots on and finishing dressing.

The girl was still huddled naked and miserable on the dirty floor of the bare little room, but he made no attempt to comfort or to reassure her now.

Skye Fargo felt too empty at the sudden loss of the Ovaro to think about anything or anyone else right now.

He looked toward the window, toward the unseen and now distant riders, and the look he sent after them would have chilled the nerves of a rattlesnake.

However far those men went, wherever they tried to hide, the Trailsman figured to find them.

Whatever it took, whatever the cost, whatever the coin, time, or sweat, or blood, he would spend it.

2

Fargo reached for the bolt on the door, then stopped. He was dressed now and ready to go, so preoccupied with the needs of the moment that he wasn't even aware of Margarita, who continued to huddle on the floor next to the wall, sobbing and naked.

He closed his eyes and leaned against the doorjamb. He looked as if he had slumped against it in weariness. In fact, the Trailsman was in deep concentration. In his mind's eye he was reviewing every motion, every mannerism, and most important of all, every face and frame and horse he had seen in that street down below.

Deliberately, while the images remained fresh in his memory, he was recalling them one by one, concentrating on them with total intensity, committing each of them to memory for future recall.

He had never had the opportunity to actually see the men who had once destroyed his family. If he had, things might have been far different. There never would have been a man known as the Trailsman. There never would have been a man who went by the name "Fargo." If that had happened . . . But there was no point in speculations, he realized. It was too late to wipe out realities, no matter how harsh.

This time, though, things were different. Those men had ridden past and beneath him. He had seen each and every one of them and he didn't intend to forget any of them.

He concentrated on that, drawing on every power of observation he possessed, until he was satisfied. Then, opening his eyes and shaking himself as if he were just awakening from a deep sleep, he drew the bolt and went down the saloon stairs with a firm but unhurried stride.

The saloon was empty. Even the bartenders and the piano player had abandoned their posts to rush outside into the wake of the afternoon's excitement.

The street, however, was far from empty. People crowded in from blocks around now that the danger of the shooting was past. Most gathered as close as they could get to the body of the storekeeper who had been shot down by the fleeting gunmen.

Everyone seemed to be talking at once, each person repeating the tale to whoever would listen, and each and every one of them seemed to have the full story on exactly what had happened.

There had been five gunmen. There had been eight. The town had been raided by an armed force of twenty-six abolitionists down from Missouri. The eleven gunmen were participants in a bloody feud between two families, the feud sparked by one family's son defiling another family's daughter.

The robbers/raiders/gunmen had shot down two people, four, seven, before they made their getaway.

They were men from Missouri and Kansas and Louisiana and Mexico. Most of the people on the street quickly became convinced that the whole thing had been a raid by Mexicans trying to retake San Antonio. The city had, after all, been raided several times by military forces from the south since Texas was so bloodily split off from Mexican-government control. The famous Alamo was not three blocks away. That story gained plausibility quickly and became an accepted "fact." Yet Fargo had seen the riders. There wasn't a Mexican among them.

Before nightfall, though, it was entirely probable that men of Mexican extraction would begin to suffer, perhaps to die, in retaliation for the "raid."

Fargo listened with growing disbelief, finally was forced to conclude that he would learn nothing here. He walked east, in the direction the six gunmen had ridden from, and finally discovered the truth.

The gang had robbed a small, commercial banking firm. The two men who had been working in the bank died during the robbery, and it was impossible at this stage for anyone to know how much the robbers had gotten away with.

Fargo heard quite specific figures anyway, because there was every bit as large a crowd on that block and every bit as much excitement as there had been in the street near the saloon. The gang had stolen $1,500. $2,200. $12,000. $14,746.23. That one actually amused him. The man who told it to him was wide-eyed at the enormity of the amount and repeated it several times over, certain to the very penny.

The Trailsman took his time now, idling nearby until he could sort out the sheep from the goats. Eventually he spotted a heavyset man with bushy side-whiskers and sprinklings of cigar ash on the front of his vest. If anyone was in charge here, it seemed to be that man. He had come out into the street to speak with a tin-starred young man who was being beseiged by loud questioners. Fargo tried to follow the big man inside the bank.

"No, dammit, no visitors." Another deputy or police officer or whatever they called themselves here grabbed him by the sleeve and stopped him.

The look Fargo gave the man was chilling. The deputy flushed a dark red and snatched his hand away from Fargo's arm like he had been burned. "You can't go inside," he said mulishly.

Fargo ignored the man but didn't try to shove past. He looked at the back of the big man's head and raised his voice. "Do you want to recover the money?"

The man Fargo had been following either did not hear or chose not to respond, but a taller, slimmer gentleman standing by him did hear. That one said something to the big man, then came toward Fargo.

"What was that you said?"

Fargo took a moment to look the fellow over before he answered.

The gentleman was tall and lean, probably in his early fifties. He had streaks of silver highlighting his temples and sprinkled lightly through a mane of dark, well-barbered hair. He smelled faintly of hair tonic, and the price of his suit of clothes would have kept a family in tall cotton for a year.

"Were you speaking to us?"

Fargo nodded. "I asked were you interested in recovering whatever was stolen from here today."

The beefy man joined them. His expression wasn't welcoming. "Move along, you," he ordered.

"Wait a minute, George. Do you know something about this robbery, mister?" the gentleman asked.

"Only what I saw," the Trailsman said. "And that those sons of bitches stole my horse on their way out. My horse and saddle and most of the things I own in this world. I'm going after them anyway. I'll find them. When I do, I'll take back what's mine. I only have. . . ." He dug into his pocket and pulled out a scant handful of coins. "I only have fourteen dollars and change to my name, thanks to those boys. I'll get onto them quicker if I can get somebody to stake me to a horse and gear. If I catch up with them soon enough, they won't have had a chance to divide your money and spend so much of it

21

first. If you want to give me that stake, mister—and I'm assuming you have something to do with this bank that was robbed—I'll agree to bring back what's yours when I bring back what's mine. Simple deal."

The big man snorted and chewed on an unlighted cigar stub. "Get out o' here before I have you arrested on suspicion of bein' part of that gang, mister. And take your hard-luck story with you. My boys'll have that bunch in wrist irons before you go to bed tonight."

Fargo smiled at him. "If you say so. I'll be pleased to be proved wrong."

"Even if you was right, mister, I can't see any reason why Harry would want to trust some damn-fool drifter in off the streets when he has my fine boys to catch those thieves for him."

"Is there a reason why we should trust you if the posse fails?" the tall gentleman asked.

Fargo shrugged and smiled again. "I saw those boys ride out. They weren't set up for a long haul. They'll be dragging back in here before dawn, and the only thing they'll bring with them is a big thirst for some free whiskey while they tell their stories. Your money won't be with them."

"You act awfully sure of yourself."

"I am," Fargo said simply.

"Go on now," the big man named George said. "Get out of here."

Fargo ignored George, who he assumed would be either the sheriff or the town marshal, and looked directly into the eyes of the gentleman called Harry. "My name is Fargo. Some call me the Trailsman. You ask around about that, Harry. Then, when you want to hire me to recover your money—my price will be a horse and gear, no more—you look me up. I've a room on the second floor of Linderman's." He smiled. "I'll expect to see you after the posse gets back."

"Get out of here, Fargo," George said. "We have

more important things to do than listen to the likes of you."

Fargo touched his hat brim to Harry but ignored George. He turned and walked away from the bank, heading back toward the saloon.

The room was paid for. That had happened before he became suddenly broke. The proceeds from his last employment were hidden in his saddlebags.

He had no other place to go.

But then he was in no hurry now. He had to wait for Harry to come look him up.

The knock on Fargo's door came shortly after midnight. He'd been expecting it. He'd seen the tired posse members dragging in about a half-hour earlier— empty-handed, as he had predicted, and with several of their horses limping and one pair of men riding double. So there had been some rough going wherever that gang had led them. Fargo didn't believe for a minute that the posse had gotten close enough to the gang to get into a gunfight with them. His guess after watching them leave was that George's "boys" just weren't good enough to get so close to the robbers.

"Who is it?" he answered through the door, although he had a pretty damn good idea of who it had to be.

"Harry Burton, Mr. Fargo."

"Door's open. Come on in." Fargo waited to see that it was indeed the tall gentleman from the bank and that Burton was alone before he uncocked the Colt and dropped it back into the holster hanging at the head of the bed.

"You are a cautious man, Mr. Fargo," Burton observed as he closed the door behind him.

"Pays to be, Mr. Burton." Fargo motioned Burton toward the lone chair in the shabby room. "Should I bother asking about the robbers your friend George is supposed to have in wrist irons by now?"

"I am here," Burton said. "That should be answer enough."

Fargo nodded. "And so it is, sir."

"I have been thinking about your proposition, Mr. Fargo. Or should I call you Trailsman? I did as you suggested. I asked about that too. You have the reputation of being a rough customer at times. But an honest one. I am told that you will see a thing through."

Fargo nodded again. "No point in starting a thing if you're just gonna quit it before it's over."

"It is only fair to tell you that George Samson advises me against accepting your offer. He feels that his men, given reprovisioning and a fresh start . . ."

Fargo grinned at him. "What are you, Mr. Burton? President of the bank? Owner?"

"Both," Burton admitted.

"I don't think you got to where you are, Mr. Burton, by betting on slow horses as long shots."

Burton smiled. "Hardly."

"I'm going after those fellows regardless. The thing in question is when I do it. If I have to stay here long enough to earn my stake, there's that much less chance of me recovering my horse and gear. No question that I'll get the men before I quit their trail, but it's the horse that I want. Same thing is true for your money. The longer they're spending it, the less there will be in hand when I find them."

"But you would return the money regardless, Mr. Fargo?"

Fargo shrugged. "Six months from now there could be a lot of question about what belonged to who if it takes me that long to find them."

"Six months? It could take that long?"

"Could take ten times that for all I know. If you want guarantees, Mr. Burton, go see George Samson. I don't doubt that he can give you an exact schedule of what he wants to see happen. Me, I'm not so certain about these things. If I leave San Antonio tomorrow, I might have those men back in town by sundown. But it'd be a slow-horse bet to count on that. I won't stay after them a day less than I need, nor a day longer. Beyond that, I really couldn't guess. "

Burton sighed. He crossed his legs and pulled out a slender cheroot. "Do you mind?"

"No."

"Thanks."

Fargo guessed that Burton's complicated process of getting the cheroot warmed and lighted, something you might expect to see for a fat and sassy dime cigar but not for some picayune cheroot, was a time-killer while the man came to a decision.

After a moment Burton grunted, as if to himself, and said, "George wanted me to at least provision you as cheaply as possible if I insisted on being foolish enough—his words—to place my trust in you. Which I find that I do, Mr. Fargo."

Fargo nodded. He wasn't surprised.

"Frankly, though, I believe the sensible thing for me to do will be to give you a free hand. Tomorrow morning you may choose any available horse in San Antonio. I will stand good for it. Also whatever else you need. Just have the bills sent to me at the bank. We open at eight. If you want to stop by then, I can give you a signed authorization to that effect."

"I've already picked out the horse," Fargo said. "Gave me something to do this evening. Belongs to an old fellow named Chambers. He threw in a saddle and blanket, but I will have some shopping to do before I head out."

"You were that sure of our deal?"

"Like I said, it gave me something to do for the evening. No harm done if you wanted to stick with Samson."

Burton smiled, not sure if he should believe that or not. "Chambers, you said. Wally?"

"That was the name he gave me."

"Is the horse a mare, Fargo? Big, awkward-looking thing with a neck like a snake?"

"That's the one."

"I think . . . Perhaps, since I do have a certain interest in this matter, you won't resent me saying so, but I think you should know that Wally Chambers has been trying to palm that animal off for the better part of a year. Ever since two different cowboys were badly hurt breaking her. That mare has a bad reputation and a worse disposition, Mr. Fargo. She is mean through and through."

"Uh huh. That's the horse, all right," Fargo said pleasantly.

"Well?"

"Well, what?"

"Do you still want a horse that you know is bad?"

"I want a horse that's tough, Mr. Burton. I'm not taking her to keep company with. That one there looks like the toughest thing in San Antonio, and that's exactly what I want from her."

Burton looked unconvinced, but he didn't argue the point further.

Which was just as well. Harry Burton was not the one who would be expected to go out and capture six gunmen. Skye Fargo was.

He corrected himself: six gunmen, only if that one decent shot he'd gotten off hadn't been a disabling one. It could well be five men that he was after by now, depending.

Burton stood and offered his hand. Fargo took it. That was all the contract the Trailsman required. He was committed now to the recovery of the bank's money as well as his own Ovaro.

There was only one thing that could keep him from fulfilling that handshake deal.

And he did not really expect to die soon.

*　　*　　*

Fargo didn't bother trying to sort out the tracks of the gang as he rode west from San Antonio. Everything readily identifiable would have been obscured within minutes after the disappearance of the gang around that street corner, wiped out or covered over by the crowds of people who raced for the bloody scene as quickly as the danger was past.

Besides, Fargo didn't need to identify them. The Ovaro was with them. And he knew the big, black-and-white horse's hoofprint as well as he knew his own face in the morning's shaving mirror. Better. He saw those tracks far more often than he had occasion to look into a mirror.

He frowned and looked down toward the neck and ears of the brown mare he was riding now.

She was a damn ugly thing. No one could quarrel with that statement. What was it Burton had said? Neck like a snake? That was true enough. So was the rest of her. She looked like an oversized whippet, tall and lean and said to be vicious, like a whippet gone rabid.

That was all right. Other men might see that part of her. The reason Fargo wanted her was that she also had the look of a horse that could go day and night without faltering. Her barrel was narrow but deep through the lungs. It felt strange to have such a different horse between his knees, to sit at such a strange height after so many years of feeling, knowing, the stout pinto. Her legs were long but sturdy, with round cannons and set wide at the fore. With shoulders set to a perfectly sloping angle beneath an ugly, mottled brown hide, she had wide, flaring nostrils to gather air and the endurance that came with it. She was a helluva lot of horse.

Fargo suspected, too, from her reputation, that this was one of those animals that a man could push until he killed her. But no one would ever be able to push her until she quit. There simply would be no quit in her. No more than there was in the Trailsman.

27

She was not the Ovaro. But she would do to help him recover that fine horse.

The trail the posse had taken lay partially over the tracks of the robbers. Both were easy to pick up once he got beyond the busy environs close to the town, but Fargo had no interest in staying directly with either set of tracks.

He had seen the condition of the posse members' horses when they returned last night. He had looked more closely this morning while he was waiting for the bank to open. Several would be disabled for weeks or longer by the deep thorns driven into their joints. The livery hostler had told him that one posseman lost his horse and nearly lost his life as well in a nighttime fall off the lip of a cutbank where the gang had led them.

The robbers had known exactly where they were going when they made their dash out of town. They had planned and prepared for the pursuit. Whoever was leading them was no pilgrim. The man knew what he was doing and did it well.

The gang would know that the posse had turned back. It was unlikely that they could suspect that the Trailsman was behind them. They could reasonably be expected to lower their guard now. Enjoying the sensations of freedom and victory with their saddlebags crammed with the bank's money, they would slow down and relax, secure in the knowledge that there was no longer a posse behind.

Let them, Fargo thought. The more they relaxed, the slower they chose to travel now, the better he would like it.

His lips twisted in a thin smile.

The men couldn't yet know what a mistake they had made when they grabbed for the reins of that particular tied horse on the street. Skye Fargo intended to inform them of that mistake.

He trotted the ugly mare to the top of a low hill and stopped there.

The country north and west of San Antonio was known as the Hill Country of Texas, and with good reason. It was a pretty land of rolling hills, grass over much of the surface and studded with cedar. Thick denser growth lay in the bottoms and along the occasional streams. There was cactus in a thousand varieties in the dry places, where the thin soil covered hard rock. Gray outcroppings of pale stone marked the sides and tops of many of the endless hills.

The gang must have led the posse to and through a number of those, but Fargo felt no reason to follow blindly in a track made deliberately difficult. Better by far to determine where the gang seemed to be going and head there by the easiest, quickest possible route.

He scouted the posse's trail from afar, riding wide around the difficult areas and taking his time about it.

He found the place where the posse had turned back during the night. In daylight it was far from intimidating, but at night, unable to see the surrounding terrain, it must have been rugged.

The body of the posseman's dead horse, saddle and bridle stripped from it, was at the bottom of a drop of eighteen or twenty feet from an eyebrow trail that squeezed tightly between the edge of the cutbank and a thick clump of cedar and chaparral. A single misstep had been enough to send the horse falling to its death from a broken neck. The rider had been dumb-lucky to have survived with no worse than bruises.

Fargo shook his head. A dozen yards away, on the other side of the cedar clump, there was easy passage that the posse could have taken to avoid the danger point. But it had been night. In the heady excitement of the chase they hadn't bothered to take the time to look for a safe route.

Still shaking his head over the ignorance of George Samson's possemen, Fargo rode closer. The robber gang hadn't been so foolish. They had taken the easy, safe

29

detour through the rocks. The posse had held blindly to the narrow game trail they had been following for more than a mile. The misjudgment had cost them the chase. Others in the party had gone no farther than to follow the game or cattle trail down into the wash below, before turning back to help the downed rider.

Foolish, Fargo thought, but no more so than he would have expected. The robbers had certainly known what they were doing here.

He took the ugly brown mare to the lip of the wash and looked down into it. There was little enough to see. Coyotes had been at the dead horse during the night. One of the possemen had lost a belt knife in the sandy bottom. Its blade glittered in the sunlight.

Fargo didn't bother to ride down to claim the thing. He turned the brown away, back toward the trail the gang had taken. The horse took that opportunity to balk. She turned that thin, snaky neck and tried to remove the Trailsman's toes with her snapping teeth. She had been on good behavior all morning.

She went back to that good behavior when Fargo reacted with a sharp kick that mashed her upper lip against her strong, yellowed teeth.

The horse turned and trotted obediently in the direction he gave her, acting as if nothing at all had happened. Fargo sat loose and easy in the unfamiliar saddle that Chambers had thrown in on the deal.

The trail was easy enough to follow. Obviously the gang had been listening out in the darkness, taking their time. Sure of themselves against the inexperienced posse members, they had waited quietly from a safe distance, then made camp within rifle range of the last point the possemen had reached and built themselves a fire.

Cheeky sons of bitches, Fargo thought, but good at what they did.

That in itself was a rarity. Tales of dashing desperadoes

to the contrary, the plain truth was that most criminals turned out to be dumb bastards, too lazy and unreliable to make a living at a regular job and stupid enough to genuinely believe that they wouldn't be caught, that they could prey on the weak and the wealthy and get away with it forever simply because they were daring and immortal.

That was bullshit, of course. Anyone with gumption enough to spit in a robber's eye and bash the son of a bitch over the head could put the fear into the average rowdy on a rampage.

This crowd, though, seemed different—professionals at thievery and at escape. They were cool, confident, and sharp enough to get away with it.

They used all the usual tricks as a matter of course: choosing their route to follow rock whenever possible, then changing direction once they got their horses onto the hard surface; mixing their tracks into those of cattle whenever they chanced onto a group of the half-wild ladinos that inhabited this excellent but sparcely populated grazing country.

The myriad small tricks they employed would have put off the pursuit of most posses, and these men were making no assumptions that they were running free and clear just because that first hurriedly assembled bunch had turned back.

Fargo gave them credit where it was due. But it would have taken a hell of a lot more than those simple things to hide their passage from him. He read their trail as easily as a banker reads the latest stock-market reports.

Besides, he didn't have to follow directly in their tracks. To find them he had only to determine their direction of travel and check every so often to make sure they hadn't deviated from it.

They were riding west. So did Fargo, the hoofprints of the black-and-white Ovaro pinto clear every time he found their trail.

The gang had a long lead over him when they started, but the Trailsman was able to close that gap quickly. They continued to take the time to make little swings and detours to discourage tracking, while Fargo was able to move straight ahead on the westward course.

By the afternoon of his second day he figured they were less than half a day ahead of him.

Then he swung around one of the countless low, cedar-covered hills, and the game became more serious.

3

"Damn," Fargo said aloud. The brown horse pinned its ears flat at the sound of the human voice and made a pass at his foot with bared teeth. The teeth failed to connect, and Fargo ignored the horse. He had other things to think about at the moment.

A cabin—or what remained of one—lay fifty yards away. The rock walls were standing, but the pole-and-sod roof had collapsed. Wisps of smoke from the smoldering remains of a fire drifted above the blackened walls and were driven south by the fresh breeze.

A pole corral nearby stood empty, its gate torn down and the gatepost broken.

The tracks of the gang's horses, the Ovaro among them, led into the ranch yard.

"Damn," Fargo said again. He booted the brown mare none too gently and rode forward. He tied the horse to one of the remaining corral rails and took a moment to loosen the cinches of the rimfire Texas saddle.

While he was doing that, his back to the smoldering cabin, there was a flurry of movement behind him. He turned to see a girl charging across the beaten earth of the yard, torn skirts flying around her thin legs and an iron poker upraised to strike him across the back of the head.

Fargo stepped away from the mare, as there was no sense in allowing a stray blow to make the already skittish bitch even more so, and let the girl commit herself with a wild swing of the potentially lethal poker.

As soon as the weapon was in motion, Fargo ducked inside the sweep of her arm, blocked it, and plucked the poker out of her hand. "Whoa now."

The girl ignored him. She was blinded by tears and fright and anger, and probably never heard him speak. With no poker to hit him with, she began kicking and bawling and trying to scratch his eyes with hooked fingers and broken nails.

"Whoa now," Fargo repeated. He stepped behind the terrified but nonetheless furious girl, captured her wrists, and pinned her arms to her sides.

She continued to struggle, trying to stomp him, although she was barefoot and her heels had no effect on his boots.

"Calm down, miss. I don't aim to hurt you. Just settle yourself now. Please."

She was trembling with either fury or fear. After a moment more she fainted dead away.

"Shit," Fargo mumbled. He bent and scooped her dead weight into his arms, then stood looking around wondering what in hell to do with her now that he had her.

There would be nothing left inside that cabin, but on the south side of the fire-riven house he could see a ring of stone wall that would mark the homestead's well. He carried her to it and knelt to lay her gently onto a patch of lush grass that grew where the spills and overflows from buckets of drawn water had fallen. There was no shade, but the soft grass gave an impression of cool relief from the heat of the sun.

Fargo wanted to bathe the feisty girl's face, but there

was no sign of bucket or hoist. He looked down into the well. A wooden bucket lay partially submerged in the water twenty feet below. Its rope was still attached to the bail, but someone had thrown the rope down into the well along with the bucket.

"I didn't really figure to go fishin' today," Fargo muttered to the unconscious girl.

There might be something inside the ruined cabin that he could use to recover the rope and bucket or even a spare bucket and some cord he could use. He checked the girl. She was still out. It would do no harm to leave her for a moment. He went toward the cabin. The door, a frame of pegged and tied poles covered with rawhide, had been ripped off the leather hinges and was lying in the dirt of the yard. Someone had done a job on this place.

Fargo stepped inside, his eyes stinging from the smoke that eddied inside the walls, and stopped short.

Someone was whimpering and groaning. At the back of the cabin, he thought, buried now under the poles and sod that had fallen into the place during the fire.

The unconscious girl forgotten for the moment, the Trailsman began to pull chunks of dry, fire-cured sod off the mess that had been the roof, throwing them out the front door and prizing free the cedar poles as he came to them.

Whoever was under the roof was hurting bad and might not last much longer if the smoke was reaching him down there.

Lordy, but there was a ton of the shit. Maybe more. He bent and hauled and heaved and threw the stuff out until it felt like his back was going to break. But there was no time to waste. If he didn't get the weight of the poles and sod off, and get the fellow out of the lingering smoke, it was going to be too late. Fargo worked as quickly as he dared, balancing the necessity for speed against the kind of foolish hurrying that could make a man make a mistake. If he pulled the wrong beam out in his haste, it was possible he might remove a prop and dump even more sod onto the poor man. Fargo grunted as he worked and quickly was running sweat.

The girl, revived without Fargo's help, came in through the shattered door.

"Good," he said. "You can hel—"

She had that damn poker again, and for the second time that afternoon she tried to brain him with it.

This time Fargo was too exasperated to bother being nice about it. He chopped her wrist so hard he might have broken it, snatched the poker out of her hand, and hurled it over the stone walls toward the back of the cabin.

"Will you quit this bullshit?" he complained. "There's somebody buried under what used to be a roof here, and if we don't get him out pretty soon, it might be too late. Now either give me a hand with clearing this away or stand back so's I can do it without worrying what you're up to."

The girl colored. "I thought . . ."

"Little lady, I don't give a damn what you thought. Now which are you going to do? Help out or make me tie you up so you won't be in the way?"

She gave him a dirty look and snapped, "So I made a mistake. Big deal. That's no reason for you to be wasting time like this." She bent and began hauling at the half-burnt timbers with soot-blackened hands. He guessed that she had been trying to remove the rubble by herself when he arrived and interrupted the job.

Fargo bent to the chore too. The work went much faster with the two of them tackling it together.

The girl was a little bit of a thing. He guessed she would be fourteen, maybe fifteen. Certainly not big enough to have much in the way of a figure yet. She was covered with dirt and sweat and ash and soot so that it wasn't particularly easy to see what it looked like. Not that it mattered. Fargo wasn't the kind of man to be having that sort of thought about young ones.

Little as she was, she was a worker, though. She was willing to grab on to the biggest, heaviest thing in sight and wrestle it to a finish.

"Let me get those big ones," he said.

"I can manage."

"Hell yes, you can manage them, but it takes you three times as long as it ought to. I can get those while you clear out the sod strips."

Her first reaction was a frown, but after a moment she accepted the logic of what he said. After that, with the two of them operating more or less as a team, the work of clearing out the mess went much quicker.

The victim trapped underneath it all was still alive, but the moans and groans were weaker than they had been.

After half an hour of hard labor Fargo said, "He's right back there. I can see his shirt, I think."

The girl looked where Fargo was pointing and nodded.

"If you can raise up on this pole right here, I can crawl under and drag him out, I think."

The girl took another moment to assess the problem, then said, "You can get that thing higher an' hold it longer'n I could. You lift. I'll get him out."

"That's too dangerous. If I slip . . ."

"Damnation, mister. Just do it, okay?" Before he could respond she was bellydown on the packed-earth floor and already wriggling forward, trying to worm her way under the heavy and dangerously loose debris.

It was her neck, and she seemed to know what she was risking. Fargo took a good hold on the long piece of timber he had pointed out to her, braced himself, and pushed up, using his legs to get a good drive and lifting with his arms as well.

Son of a bitch, that beam was heavy. Smaller poles and several hundredweight of sod were lying on it. If he slipped . . . Better not to think about that. Better to concentrate on not slipping while two live people were under there.

The muscles in Fargo's arms corded. The strain of it ran all through him, trying to press his spine into a compact column of fused bone and sinew. It cramped his legs, and sweat made his hands slippery.

"Could you please hurry?" His voice was raw and rasping. In addition to the effort of trying to hold the beam up, the damn smoke was getting to him. It continued to leak off the partially burned wood and the long-dried grass and roots of the sod.

"I almost . . . I have him," the girl said triumphantly. "Hold on. I just need to . . . brace . . . there."

Fargo heard her grunt with effort. He could hear something move, grating across the floor. Then the beam he was holding felt suddenly lighter as something slipped off it and fell with a loud crash.

"Damn!" It was the girl's voice.

"Are you all right?"

"Yeah. Just a minute now. I have to get a fresh hold." She pulled again. "I moved him, mister. I moved him. Can you raise up a bit more?"

Fargo braced the end of the beam against his thigh, took a new grip on the wood, and gave it everything he had left. He was able to raise the end of the pole perhaps eight or ten inches more, which would be very little improvement down at the other end of it where the girl was.

"Hold it there," she called. "Just a little more now."

There was a moment of silence, then a few loud grunts, finally a cry of "Got him!"

Fargo could see her wiggling back out from under the pile of debris, dragging the limp, unconscious form of a man with her. The hem of her dress hiked high as she crawled backward, exposing her legs all the way up to her butt.

She wasn't wearing any underpants, and Fargo discovered all too clearly that while she might be damned young, she was plenty old enough to have a pertly rounded, dimple-cheeked rear end. He felt ashamed of the erection he could feel pushing at the buttons of his fly, but he seemed unable to do anything about that.

Certainly she wasn't thinking in terms of maidenly modesty at the moment. She was concentrating on dragging the injured man free of the jumbled wood and sod. She seemed to be pulling mostly with one hand and favoring the other. She must have hurt herself while she was under there. No help for that now.

Fargo could feel the sweat-slippery beam begin to twist in his tired hands, and there was damn little he could do to stop it.

"You'd best hurry. I'm fixing to . . . lose . . . this . . . damn. . . ."

The girl dragged the injured man's legs free, and with a sigh of relief Fargo let go of the beam. It and everything piled on top of it fell to the floor with an earsplitting crash, and dust and smoke filled the roofless cabin until the gusts of breeze overhead could suck some of it away over the walls.

The girl was paying no attention to Fargo. She was kneeling beside the man, who was clean-shaven and gray-haired, probably in his fifties. He was a lean, poorly dressed fellow. Fargo guessed him to be the owner of this hardscrabble homestead.

Skye knelt beside the girl. She was running her palm over the man's cheeks and forehead and crooning to him without words, just soft, low sounds of comfort, letting him know that she was there and that he was safe now.

That was all well and good, of course, but it told them nothing about how the man was hurt. There was blood on the front of his shirt, bright scarlet fresh against the filth of soot and dirt from all that debris that had pinned him. Fargo didn't bother unbuttoning the shirt. He just yanked it open, sending a spray of buttons off to one side as the thread gave way.

"Uh oh," Fargo said.

The girl looked at him without comprehension.

"That isn't a puncture from a stick or something. He's been shot." He pointed to the wound. It was a small, almost harmless-looking damp red circle just above and to the left of the breastbone.

"He'll be all right, won't he?"

"I couldn't say," the Trailsman told her.

That was, in fact, a lie. He could have said. He didn't want to. He was assuming that this girl must be the wounded man's daughter, and he didn't want to give her any more pain than was going to be necessary. Besides, no man is infallible. He could be wrong. The bright-pink froth that was forming bubbles over the tiny entry wound meant it had been a lung shot. But, hell, maybe the guy would survive it. Somehow. Fargo wouldn't lay any money on it, but anything was possible. One man might get shot through the head and live, while his neighbor could get stung by a bee and die. There weren't any guarantees.

But if Fargo had to guess, he would have had to say that this man was on his way out.

"Is there a spare bucket?" Fargo asked. "Or anything I could use to hook the rope and bucket out of the well? We'll want to clean him up and do what we can for him. We'll need water."

"Stay here with him. I'll get it."

Fargo raised an eyebrow toward her.

"I used to drop the damn rope all the time. I can climb down in and bring the rope back. I've done it ten dozen times since we came here. I won't be but a minute."

"All right."

The girl left and Fargo used the privacy to take a closer look at the wounded man.

He hadn't only been shot. He had been beaten too. His hands had been tied with strong cord, but the cord had later been cut. Both wrists were still tied with it.

The man was pretty far gone, Fargo judged. Maybe

too far for him to even know that they had gotten him clear or that his girl was there to tend and care for him.

Fargo hoped that for the man's comfort and peace of mind he might at least have that much awareness left.

The girl came back, hauling the heavy water bucket with her, the hem of her dress dripping wet and her feet bare. She dropped to her knees beside her father and began to bathe his face with a scrap of cloth she produced from somewhere.

They cleaned the dying man and made him as comfortable as it was going to be possible to make him, carrying him to the patch of grass by the well where Fargo had earlier laid the girl. Fargo asked her what had happened. She began telling it like it was a story. Or something that had happened to someone else and she had heard about it. Certainly she was displaying none of the emotions that he would have expected.

"There were six of them," the girl said in a dull, almost disinterested tone of voice. "I was just coming back from taking a bath. Norman was in the house. He was cutting rawhide into strips to use for making a new riata. He said his old one was wearing out." She paused and looked toward the man—Norman apparently—who lay on the grass taking his time about his dying.

Six of them, she said. He had expected that, of course. The gang had taken time out for a bit of play here. Happy boys out on a lark now that their saddlebags were stuffed with stolen money. Damn them.

"They stopped to water their horses," she said. "I suppose they would have done that, and that would have been the end of it. They would have ridden away and left us alone, except that I'd just had my bath and hadn't bothered to dry off very well. My dress was clinging to me. That excited them. They wanted to rape me." She said that just as tonelessly, just as matter-of-factly as she had related the fact that they wanted to water their horses.

"Norman got very angry. He objected. There were words. Accusations. Threats. You know."

Fargo nodded. That he could understand. It was the girl's distant attitude that he failed to understand.

"Norman went inside. We have—had—a rifle and a shotgun and some pistols. He went to get them. One of the men shot him. All of them laughed. They thought it was funny, and it amused them that Norman was still alive. They held him upright and made him watch while they took turns having me. All of them except the one with the bandages."

So he had wounded that one, Fargo thought with satisfaction. The son of a bitch was suffering then. Good.

"They took turns. They wanted to torment Norman. They kept looking at Norman and laughing.

"All that was inside the house. When they were done, they took what they wanted, mostly food and Norman's guns, and they shoved him back into the corner. He was too weak by then to do anything anyway. And one of them, his name was Mickey or maybe Mikey, something like that anyway, he said he would shoot me if the others wanted. They all agreed to that and carried the things they'd taken, went out to the horses with them. I could hear them tearing down the corral gate and driving our saddle horses out. They stole them too, of course."

Fargo nodded but didn't interrupt. She was telling it just fine, still without showing any emotion over any of it.

"The one named Mickey winked at me and fired his revolver into the ceiling. That's what started the fire. They didn't bother to do it deliberately. It was when that Mickey shot into the ceiling instead of me. He winked at me—did I tell you that already?—he winked at me and whispered, 'You 'member this if the time comes.' Then he laughed and looked at Norman. I thought he was going to shoot Norman again, but he didn't. He laughed and chucked me under the chin and went outside with the rest of them. I don't think he ever saw that the roof was burning. There wasn't much smoke to begin with. The underneath poles were dry, you understand, and didn't give off much smoke. And then I heard them ride off.

"I went out to make sure they were gone. I tried to get a bucket of water to throw on the roof, but one of them must have dropped the rope after they watered their horses. And I was climbing down inside the well to get it when I heard Norman scream. The fire had gotten bad by then. I climbed back out and tried to get him. You know, drag him outside. But by then the fire had caught and was really bad. The roof fell in. I had time enough to jump out of the way, but it came down on top of Norman. I could hear him. Like when you got here but stronger. He was awfully scared. I was still inside trying to pull the mess off him when I heard you come and thought you were one of them coming back for something. That's why I grabbed the poker and tried to bash you, mister. I'm sorry about that. I really am."

It occurred to Fargo that they had never gotten around to introductions. He gave her his name.

"Pleased to meet you, Mr. Fargo," she said formally. "I'm Jane. He's Norman. Norman Walters."

"Pleased to meet you, Miss Walters."

She gave him an odd look. "I'm not a Walters."

"Not . . . ? Isn't Norman Walters your dad?"

She shook her head solemnly. "No, I'm just Jane. Never got around to taking a last name, an', of course, nobody knows what it ought to have been."

Fargo was definitely puzzled now. "If you aren't his daughter, then who?"

"That's right. You aren't from around here, or I expect you'd know."

"I don't know what you mean."

Still in that emotionless tone she said, "I'm a sort of foundling, I guess you could say. Comanch' stole me

43

when I was a baby, raised me for a while." She paused and checked on Norman again.

"As I got older, I was everybody's girl. Five or six years, I guess." So she was somewhat older than she looked. Had to be, Fargo thought. "Then they were having a bad year. The game was scarce, and the Mexicans below the river where they used to raid for grain and women and such, they were having a bad year too, and the man that owned me then swapped me at one of the missions over to San Antonio for an ox and some fat burros. Hard times like that, meat's more important than a woman. They could still raid the Mexicans for women even if there wasn't much grain. So they traded me off, and Norman and his missus took me in to help Margaret with the chores. She was poorly and needed someone to help with her work. And whatever I could do to help Norman with the stock too, as I could ride just fine after being with the Comanch'.

"Then a while back, Margaret died, and after that Norman took me into his bed. That was kinda nice." She sounded wistful, pleased, about having been able to sleep in a bed. It was the most emotion she had yet shown during her tale.

She shrugged. "That's over now, of course. But Norman's a pretty good man. He never ever beat me. Not even once, though I used to do some awful dumb things until I got used to living in a white household."

She didn't say so, but Fargo got the impression that she considered that to be quite a marvel. Helluva life this girl called Jane had lived.

Again she shrugged, dismissing the memories. "Norman's dying, ain't he?"

"Yes, I think he is."

"He had some money buried inside the house. Those men never found it. Never thought to ask about it or I'd guess Norman would have told them where it was. It's over two hundred dollars, Mr. Fargo. That's a lot of money, isn't it?"

"Yes, Jane, that's a lot."

"Tell you what, Mr. Fargo. I know where it is. I'll get it for you and give you all of it for that horse of yours."

"Surely you can get to a settlement or to a neighbor's . . ."

"Ain't going to a settlement nor a neighbor, either one," she said with quiet conviction. "I'm going after those men, Mr. Fargo. I been comfortable here with Norman, and those men took that away from me. Only home I've ever had, and they took it right away from me. I'm goin' after them."

"You can't do that, Jane. Why—"

"Don't matter what you say, Mr. Fargo. I'm going. If I got to walk after them, I'm going."

"You'd die if you tried to walk after them, Jane. You—"

She interrupted him again. She snorted. "Huh. I walked most o' the years I was with the Penatekas. That's the band of the Comanch' I was with, and they wouldn't often let me use a horse. Why, I've walked all over this country, across the Llano Estacado an' down clear to Mexico. This whole country. Besides, I know where those men are headed. I heard them talkin', which they did free enough as they thought I wouldn't be alive when they left anyhow. I know where they're going, and I sure hell got nothing better to do. So I think I'll just go after them. But I sure would like to buy that horse of yours. It'd be easier if I had a horse."

"You don't have to go after them. I'm already doing that." Fargo explained his mission.

"I remember that horse. The little man with the two guns is riding that pinto."

"Not the wounded man?" Fargo asked.

"Naw. I expect the wounded one is gonna die. They put him on the poorest horse they had. Of course, they got Norman's horses too now. But the mean little one with the two guns is riding the pinto. I remember the man an' the horse both. Real well."

"Where are they headed?" Fargo asked.

The girl gave him a tight-lipped smile. "I won't be telling you that, Mr. Fargo. But I will show you."

"Jane . . . please. You have to understand—"

"No, Mr. Fargo. You're the one that's got to understand. I'm going after them. I know where, and I know how to get there. I'll tell you something more. You don't know, an' likely they don't know neither, where the water can be found between here an' there. But I do. I been there before, to every one of them hidden tanks. When I was with the Penatekas I been there. And I remember every one o' them. I can get there where maybe you can't. Unless you got me along to show you." She looked smug.

"I'll have to think about that," Fargo said.

"You better think about it real careful then, because I heard that little one say that he figured to leave no useful water behind them. Just in case there's a posse still interested in chasing them. Without me to find the water that they don't know about, Mr. Fargo, it's you would be the one to die behind them. Not me."

Fargo looked at her closely. He tried to decide if she was telling the truth or not. But there was no way he could be sure. Her expression gave away nothing. Nothing at all.

"I'll think about it," he repeated.

Jane shrugged. "We got until Norman dies. Wouldn't be decent to go off and leave him to die alone an' no one here to bury him. I'll wait until then. Then I'm going. Be easier if we go together, but it don't matter all that much. My mind's made up on it."

"You're entitled to that," Fargo admitted. He took another look at Norman Walters. The man was pale, his face and forehead beaded with cold sweat. He seemed to be unconscious now. He probably wouldn't waken again. The question was how long it would take Walters to die and whether Fargo should take the time to wait it out with Jane and help her bury Norman before he set out in pursuit of the gang, with or without the girl.

He stood, leaving her sitting cross-legged on the ground beside the dying Norman. "You say there's a place where a person can get a bath close by?"

She nodded. "Pool. Up the valley a ways there. It stands water the year 'round. You go ahead if you want. I'll wait until Norman dies. I'd just get dirty burying him otherwise. Are you taking me with you?"

"I don't know," he admitted. "I'm still thinking about it."

4

Norman Walters clung to life until well past dark. He never wakened again, had no chance to say a final farewell to the girl he died trying to protect.

"How old are you, Jane?" Fargo asked.

"Oh, I don't know for sure. Eighteen. Maybe twenty. Somewhere in there." She was busy sewing Norman Walters' body into a charred blanket they had salvaged from the cabin, and she didn't bother to look up from her chore. The light for her work was provided by an open fire built in what had been the ranch yard. There was little left in or of the cabin that would be usable.

"You look younger," Fargo said. He was resting from the work of digging a grave in the soft soil down by the nearly dry creek.

"That's because I'm so small," she said. "I never got much to eat when I was little." Again it was said as a simple statement of fact, without rancor or bitterness toward the Comanches who had held her as their slave. "Maybe that has something to do with it. I wouldn't know. Never grew much an' never got much hair down here or caught a baby." She was pointing toward her crotch. To demonstrate what she meant, she flipped the hem of her dress up to expose herself quite calmly to Fargo's view.

She was right. She was practically hairless there, only a few strands of scant hair on her pubis.

Even so Fargo's reaction was instant and instinctive. He became erect, both at the sight of her and at the memory of her shapely rump. She wasn't particularly big on modesty. But then with the Comanche she would have been accustomed to frequent bathing done virtually in public.

She smiled when she saw the bulge in his trousers. "I see your problem there, Mr. Fargo. Help me get Norman buried, and then we'll have the time. If you don't mind waiting, though, I'd like to get a bath first. I'm still soot and sweat all over."

Fargo wasn't sure if he should blush. He settled for remaining silent.

Jane finished sewing Walters into his shroud, and Fargo dragged the body to the grave he had prepared. He lowered the form into it as gently as he could and asked, "Is there anything you want to say over him?"

"I don't know the words for what he would've wanted, but . . ." She paused a moment, then stood with her arms upraised and began a low, guttural chant. Some Comanche rite, Fargo figured. It probably was the only burial ceremony she could know. It would have to do.

When she was done, she bent and began to shove dirt in on top of the still, blanket-covered form of Norman Walters. Fargo helped her. They mounded the grave and covered it with small rocks in the futile but customary attempt to discourage visits by small animals.

"Was he a Christian?" Fargo asked, thinking he could fashion a wooden cross if that would be appropriate.

"I don't know," Jane said. "He used to say 'God damn' a lot. Does that mean anything?"

"Uh, probably not." A plain marker then. He could carve Walters' name on it while the girl bathed.

"I won't be long," she said.

No, she wasn't modest. She stripped her dress off over her head and dropped it near the fire, standing naked in the popping, flickering firelight.

Fargo had to admit that he liked what he saw. She was small, but she was damned nicely put together. Very sleek and compact, as lithe and lean as a lynx, she was downright fetching. Her belly was flat and her breasts perky and firm if somewhat on the small side, with very pale, very small nipples. She was quite thin. Her ribs showed plain under tight-stretched flesh, and there was a distinct gap between the tops of her thighs. The lips of her sex were prominent. His erection returned, more insistent than ever.

The girl walked toward the pool where Fargo had bathed earlier, and he began to work out the rationalizations for himself.

It was dark. Too dark to get on the trail again before morning, even though the distance between himself and the gang had widened immensely during the afternoon while he was waiting to help bury Norman Walters.

Since he couldn't leave until morning anyway . . . The girl had suggested herself that she give him what he wanted. Needed, at this point. Damn well needed.

She was willing, and not unattractive, although he had yet to see her with her face washed and her hair clean. She would be thinking that that would help convince him to take her with him when he left in the morning.

During the past few hours he had come to a decision about that. And not one that she would like.

With only the one horse it would be impossible for him to take her along even if he wanted to saddle himself with a girl while on a killing chase. The Trailsman figured to have no trouble at all following and finding the gang of robbers, wherever they were headed. He would follow the pinto from one pole to the other if that was what it took.

As for water, if those gunmen could find it, so could he. And probably more than they would be able to locate. They wouldn't be damn fools enough to poison standing water in dry country, no matter what the girl said to try to convince him that he should take her along.

No, the only sensible thing would be to give her some advice, which she would be free to take or to reject as she pleased: tell her to head for the nearest ranch or town and to take Norman Walters' money along with her. Two hundred dollars would be enough to give her a start. She would manage.

But the Trailsman would go on alone. It was the only reasonable thing to do.

Not that he intended to tell her that. Not quite yet anyway.

He stood and lighted a lantern that had been brought out of the house. He carried it inside the standing walls of the cabin and rummaged through the litter. Walters had had no milled lumber when he built the place of stone and poles and sod, but there was a bench that had been made by someone who knew what he was doing. One end was charred, but most of the flat surface was still usable. Fargo knocked the legs off it, went back outside to squat beside the fire and began to carve a marker for the dead rancher.

When Jane returned, she spread one of Fargo's blankets on the ground near the fire to protect her bare flesh from the sharp edges of the gravel in the hard soil, and lay down on it. She parted her legs, opening herself wide for him, and lay silently watching him, waiting for him to cover her.

Fargo sat where he was, looking at her. She was quite pretty now that she was cleaned up. Much prettier than he had realized. The firelight played softly over her body, highlighting its curves and softnesses, hiding the dips and crevices in deep shadow.

Damn, but he wanted her.

But . . . like this? So matter-of-fact? So completely one-sided? There hadn't been a word or apparently a thought about any pleasure she might have been expected to get from it.

Hell, likely she'd never gotten any measure of pleasure from the act of sex. Probably never even knew that she should. Or could.

"Well?" she asked.

"Jane, have you . . . ?"

"Have I what?"

He shook his head. "Never mind." Better to show her than to tell her about it.

He could see in the firelight that she had scrubbed herself thoroughly. She was glowing pink from the scrubbing, but he could see too that she was completely dry. Willing enough, of course, but not at all ready or receptive in all the ways that a woman should be.

He smiled at her and stood to remove his clothing. Then he joined her on the blanket.

She looked confused when he lay beside her instead of immediately covering her. "What's wrong?"

"Nothing," he assured her. "Nothing at all." He held her to him and kissed her on the mouth.

Her lips remained closed and unresponsive, her eyes wide. "What . . . ?"

"It's all right," he told her gently. He kissed her again and cupped her left breast lightly in his hand, rolling her tiny, flaccid nipple between his fingertips.

"That makes me feel . . . funny . . . inside," she said in a small voice.

Fargo smiled and kissed her again. He bent his head to lick and kiss her nipples while his hand roved lower, finding her entrance, entering it only briefly, then sliding back up to search for the little button of pleasure that was hidden nearby, virginal and unused, as virginal as the outward appearance her sparce hair gave to her sex.

"Oh!"

Fargo grinned and licked his way down across her flat stomach, flicking his tongue over and through the thin patch of hair until he found the button. He licked lightly at it, and Jane wriggled and shivered.

"That . . . What are you doing?"

"I hope I'm pleasing you." He flicked the tip of his tongue over the button again and again.

"I didn't . . . I mean, I never . . ."

"Shhh," he said. "You don't have to talk. Just be still and let me show you something rather fine."

"Oh!" Her thighs spread wider apart. But not in a dutiful, disinterested manner. Now they were opening wide, welcoming, wanting. And now the juices of her interest were showing like dewdrops on the gaping, fully receptive lips.

"I never—"

"Shhh."

Her answer this time was a sigh. One small hand stole up to stroke the back of his neck as he continued to teach her.

Fargo smiled. This girl made a good student. She was willing, even eager now.

He used his tongue on her with slow, lingering care. And the next time his palm encountered her breast, her nipples were as firm as obsidian arrow points. But much warmer.

"I didn't know."

"Shhh." He continued, slowly, allowing her the time to learn and to feel and to experience.

He built her gently toward the distant, unfamiliar peak. And when finally she reached the top and burst through the last barrier of unknowing, he was pleased.

She shuddered and quivered under his touch, her lips convulsing and clutching at the fingertip placed there. She cried out aloud with her pleasure and arched her hips up to meet him.

He gave her a moment to recover, then kissed her lightly there, again on each nipple, finally on the mouth.

Jane smiled up at him. And this time she parted her lips and kissed him back—uncertainly, inexpertly, but willing . . . and of her own accord.

She too was smiling. "That was . . . It was awful nice."

"I agree," he said gently.

"But you haven't . . ."

"Oh, I will. But there's no hurry. We have lots of time. I can show you some more. About your pleasure. If you like, about a man's pleasure. Not just the one thing you already know. There's lots more if you want to give it. Not just what a man can take but what you can give. If you want to."

"I'd like to learn that." She smiled. "For you, Mr. Fargo."

The Trailsman laughed. "Mister? I think we know each other well enough that you could call me by first name now if you like."

Jane laughed too. Then she turned shy. "You really could make me feel like that again?"

"Of course. Do you want me to show you?"

She nodded, her eyes not meeting his and a rosy blush spreading over her cheeks.

"All right. And then I'll show you some of the things you can do for me. But only if you want to. I won't mind if you'd rather not."

"I want to." She grinned. "Skye. With you." She reached up and hugged him. And for just a moment there he thought she was crying. When he looked at her again her eyes were glistening. But then that might just have been with eagerness and not with tears.

For damn sure the girl was eager.

He kissed her again, then once again bent to her, lifting her quickly this time toward the pleasures she hadn't known were possible.

Oh, yes indeed, she was eager.

Fargo smiled. He was enjoying himself every bit as much as the girl was.

He could feel her hands, searching for him, finding him, fondling him with a light, shy touch.

Skye Fargo smiled. There were worse ways to spend an evening on the trail.

The Trailsman would have preferred to slip quietly away in the dawn without waking the girl. He knew she would object to being left behind. But slipping off would have been a trifle difficult. She was sleeping in his bedroll with him. Besides, she was awake and eagerly reaching for him at the first move he made. She was definitely a light sleeper, as he was himself.

This morning he felt the press of time keenly, aware that by now the six gang members were probably already up and saddling, somewhere far ahead again.

Still, this chase more and more promised to be a long one. It wouldn't be ended in great and dramatic leaps and bounds. Not after the lead they had been able to pull on him yesterday afternoon while he and the girl waited for Norman Walters to die. There would be no harm in delaying a few more minutes with Jane.

He lay with her for a little longer, enjoying her almost as much as she seemed to enjoy him, then he quickly stood and dressed. As soon as she left the bedroll to head for the undamaged outhouse behind the cabin, he rolled his gear and packed it onto the brown mare.

"You're leaving," Jane said when she saw what he was doing.

"Got to," he told her.

"You aren't taking me with you." It was more statement than question. Her voice was small and held little hope.

"No," he admitted. "I can't."

"You need me, Skye."

"It would be dangerous. I couldn't do that to you. Not now." He softened his refusal with a slow smile and a lingering kiss on her mouth.

He had expected argument—even tears, bitterness, and recriminations: almost anything except the quiet acceptance she gave him. "All right, Skye."

That was a relief. He kissed her again and accepted her help with his final preparations.

"You won't stay for breakfast?"

He shook his head.

"Wait, then. Just a minute." She ran lightly toward the burnt-out cabin. She might not have realized it, but she presented quite a fetching sight. She had not yet bothered to dress, and her round, firm little butt was attractive, her back straight and slim. No time to be thinking about that, though. And rather little inclination after the busy exertions of last night and again this morning. There were other things on Fargo's mind now.

She was as good as her word. She was back in only moments, carrying a small cloth sack. She stopped in front of him and looked suddenly shy. Her eyes dropped away from his when she held the sack out toward him. "For you," she said.

He looked inside the bag. There was a lumpy gold-and-brown mass in it. He raised an eyebrow in inquiry.

"A good food for traveling," she explained. "You don't have to cook it. Don't have to show a fire, you see. It is like . . . I . . . used to make. Sort of. But I didn't have the usual things to make it with. This bunch is dried fruit, mostly peaches, with pecans, honey, and whatever else I could find. Norman liked it as a snack at night."

Fargo nodded and tucked the sack into his saddlebags. "I have to go now."

Still she didn't protest. She kissed him, then stepped back, and he mounted the tall brown mare.

Fargo nodded again. There were no good good-byes that could be made. Without speaking, he turned the mare away and rode west, following the route the six men had taken yesterday.

He didn't look back again, but he couldn't help thinking about the girl he was leaving alone out here.

There was no telling how far it would be to the nearest neighbors. Still, she was damn well competent. There was some food still in the cabin, and some blankets not too badly burned. She would make out. He was sure she would.

She would have to, because he couldn't take the time to tend to her.

Fargo had no idea if the Walters cabin had been the westernmost habitation on the wild Texas frontier. But if it wasn't, it couldn't have missed that distinction by much. Certainly he saw no other signs of ranches or ranching, and by midday even the occasional bunches of grazing cattle had thinned down until the only cattle he saw were rare loners hiding in the brush, as wary as wildcats. These few were true ladinos and probably hadn't been branded or claimed for generations.

It was empty country he rode through now. The brush thinned and the land became drier with every smooth pace the mare took to the west.

Even the cedar became scarce, and the only trees he saw were a few runty stragglers that managed to survive in the mostly dry streambeds.

Running creeks and surface water almost disappeared. The second night west of the Walters cabin he had to dig for water to meet the needs of himself and the horse.

He didn't make coffee that night. Aside from the simple fact that coffee made with that water would have been coffee-colored even without benefit of the beans, due to the mud that came with it, it was no longer sensible to show a fire.

The Comanches were anything but tamed—as Jane could have told him far better than even he knew—and this was the time of year when their ponies were strong from good grazing, and the tribes made their long swings throughout the country they claimed, riding fifteen hundred miles or more on a single raid, penetrating sometimes deep into Mexico. Sometimes straight through the main streets of a frontier Texas town.

Given a choice, Fargo would rather not encounter any of them, particularly at night with the mare hobbled and unsaddled. In daytime he might have a chance to outrun them. At night there was no one man who could hold off an entire Comanche raiding party and hope to keep his hair. Hell, a man captured by the Comanches was likely to lose his balls too, before his hair, and lose them while he was still alive enough to know it.

And besides the Comanches, it was also possible in this country to run into stray bands of Kiowa or even east-wandering Apache.

No, Fargo thought, for the time being he would get along nicely without the benefits of a fire at night.

He unsaddled the mare, hobbled her, and turned her loose to graze on the clumps of short grass that fought for root holds in the thin, hard soil.

He used the heavy saddle as a chair, drank the muddy water he had found within a few feet of the surface in the dry creekbed, and ate a handful of Jane's strange mixture.

The stuff was good, actually. It surprised him. He had expected something on the order of pemmican, a nourishing, fireless trail food revolting to the taste, composed largely of rancid tallow and bitter wild fruits.

The mixture the girl had come up with was downright tasty, sweet with honey and "civilized" fruits. It was a little on the dry side, but another drink of the cloudy water took care of that. He would have to thank her properly for the stuff if he ever saw her again.

The Trailsman sighed. It was unlikely he would see Jane again. Unless, of course, she was in San Antonio when he got back. He would have to go back there, naturally, after he recovered the bank's stolen money . . . and the stolen Ovaro.

He could ask after her. Someone might know what had become of her.

He smiled and slid off the saddle until he was using it as a pillow instead of a chair. He was still thinking about that, and of the pleasures he'd enjoyed with the girl, when he drifted into sleep.

5

For a moment Skye Fargo thought he'd found the robber gang before he wanted to . . . by accident and without preparation.

He was following the course of another of the many dry washes that crisscrossed the dry land, down where he wouldn't be visible to anyone who might be watching. It seemed a sensible-enough precaution in country where he had no friends and where any stranger, red or white, was apt to be an enemy.

As it turned out, though, the caution had been a bit overdone. Not only could he not be seen from the higher country around, he could see damned little himself. Too little.

He rounded a curve in the sandy bottom, riding beneath a tall cutbank, and rode into plain view of a campfire surrounded by half a dozen or more lean, rough-looking men, each one of them heavily armed. And nervous.

The men jumped when Fargo came into sight, hands flashing for revolvers and nearby rifles.

Their quick reaction was enough to spook the damn mare. The horse shied, almost unseating Fargo while he was occupied reaching for his own Colt. She couldn't get that much done, but she kept him plenty busy as she went into a fit of wild bucking. It wasn't exactly the sort of solid platform a man wanted if he were going to have to do some serious shooting.

Fortunately the boys around the campfire put their guns away and took to laughing instead of firing at the intruder.

Fargo, thoroughly furious with the unpredictable mare, managed to get enough control over his right hand to shove the Colt back into its holster so he could concentrate on the horse.

She was pitching and twisting for all she was worth, and trying to rear over backward when that failed. Fargo clubbed her between the ears with a closed fist to get her back onto four legs, then grabbed a handful of mane and rode out the storm to a sweaty, heaving-chested conclusion.

The men around the fire had been doing some loud rooting—not all of it in his favor—while the fight was in progress, and now that it was ended, he could see some money changing hands. Fargo gave them a dirty look and rode near their fire.

"Light and help yourself to the coffee," one of the grinning men invited.

Now that he had a chance to get a better look at them, Fargo could see that this wasn't the group he was chasing. He'd seen none of these men before, and there was no fine Ovaro among their ground-reined horses, although there was a red, black, and white abomination in the bunch that looked almost as tough as the stupid mare Fargo was riding.

"Thanks." He swung down from his saddle and looked for a place to tie the mare. There was nothing in the creek bottom that would reliably serve, so he had to settle for hobbling her and loosing his cinches. "Coffee sounds real welcome," he said. "I haven't had any for a couple days."

"We could spare you a bit if you've run out."

"Oh, I got the makings. Just didn't want to show a fire," Fargo said.

"I'll be damned," said the man who had made the offer. He grinned. "A sensible pilgrim. We don't see many o' those. Mostly just damn fools that think they're too special to ever lose their hair. Nice t' meet a sane man in this country for a change." Still grinning, he shoved a hand forward. "I'm Jim Nelson. These rowdy-looking sons of bitches are the rest o' Nelson's Nabobs, otherwise knowed as Company D, Frontier Battalion, Texas Rangers."

Fargo smiled and shook the man's hand. "I've heard of your rangers. Not all of it bad either. I'm pleased to meet you." He introduced himself.

"Fargo," one of the quieter rangers hunkered beside the fire said. "I've heard that name before."

"Not on a wanted list, I hope," Fargo said easily.

"Naw, I don't think it was," the ranger said seriously. He pondered it for a moment. "Call you the Trailsman, do they?"

"Some do," Fargo admitted.

The ranger grunted. None of the others said anything, but they looked like they too might have heard of Fargo before.

There were eight of them, Fargo counted now. They looked like a good crew. Fit and ready for anything that might come their way. Every one of them walked heavy with steel, and there were spare revolvers holstered on the pommels of their saddles. They looked like a crowd who could handle themselves in a fight. No wonder they felt secure enough to start a midday fire out here.

"We were kinda hoping for company," Jim Nelson said. "You aren't what we expected, but you're welcome."

"Who were you expecting?" Fargo's first thought was that these rangers might be after the same gang that he was chasing.

Nelson grinned at him. "Figured after we got our

coffee brewed an' drunk, we might drag some smoke outa that fire,"—he pronounced it fahr—"an' see if we could bait some Injuns in close."

"Oh?" Fargo was busy getting his tin cup from his saddlebags and helping himself to the pot that was boiling on the coals of a smokeless driftwood fire.

"Ayuh. Got some raiders out this way. Easier to get the sons o' bitches if we can convince them to come to us." He grinned again. "Beats ridin'."

"If you can handle that whirligig thing hanging on your belt, Mr. Trailsman, you'd be welcome to stay an' enjoy the fun," another of the rangers offered.

"If they come while I'm around, I'll try not to shoot anybody in the foot," Fargo said. "These Indians been bothersome, have they?"

"Aw, you know how it is," Nelson said casually. "This time o' year they get t' feeling perky. Come down off the damn Llano an' play. This time they caught a Mexican *carreta* train northwest o' here. Though what the silly sons o' bitches woulda been doing in that country, hell, I don't know. We wouldn't o' knowed anything about it except one o' them crawled off in the confusion an' made it in afoot to a ranch. Word got around, so we came over to see could we get in on the fun."

Fun, Fargo thought. These ranger boys had a fairly strange idea of fun if fighting Comanches was part of their definition. If they were Comanches, that is. He asked.

"Ayuh. Comanch'. They come through 'most every year." Nelson chuckled. "You'd think they'd learn to leave us Tejanos alone an' concentrate south o' the river, but they never."

"How many in the raiding party?" Fargo asked.

Nelson grinned again. "The man that got away said a hunnert or more. But then you know how that goes. We'd guess not more'n thirty, forty of 'em."

Fargo looked around him: eight rangers looking for a

scrap with thirty or more Comanches. And the Texas boys were acting like they had the poor damn Comanche outnumbered. He grinned at them.

One of the rangers, a kid who looked like he couldn't have been more than seventeen, saw the expression and may have guessed at its meaning. He smiled back at Fargo and hefted the coffeepot. "Have some more o' this, Mr. Fargo?"

"Don't mind if I do. Thanks."

The kid poured for both of them and set the pot back to the side of the coals. "Time t' add some smoke, Jim?"

"Anybody want another cup first?" Nelson offered. None of his men spoke up. "How 'bout you, Fargo? You want to get clear before we show our bait?"

"I don't expect so, but I thank you for the offer." He took another sip of the steaming hot coffee. "Damn, but this does taste good. I'm glad I ran into you boys."

"That's all right," the kid said, "unless you get greedy when the shooting starts. We wanta have some fun too."

They were a crazy bunch of bastards, Fargo thought. But he liked them.

The kid picked up some twigs of greasewood and sage that had been lying by the fire and dropped them onto the coals. Immediately there was a thin billow of gray smoke where before there had been only heat shimmering in the air above the fire. The rest of the men checked their revolvers, and several of them reached for carbines.

"You seem pretty sure that the Comanche are in the neighborhood," Fargo observed.

"That's 'cause we are," Nelson informed him. "They 'most always use the same route when they start out on their raiding. We've tracked 'em often enough. So we come down ahead of them this time. Way I figure it, they shouldn't be but a few miles away." He glanced up toward the sun. "Give 'em a bit. I calculate they'll be here."

"All right." Fargo was in no position to argue the point. This was, after all, their country. He went to the hobbled mare and pulled his Sharps out of the boot, then made sure he had ammunition for both it and the Colt and a good supply of percussion caps.

"Have some more coffee," the kid offered cheerfully. "We got some time yet."

"Thanks."

Crazy bastards, Fargo thought again.

The smoke continued to form a dark column in the clear air above the wash, a signal for anyone within miles that there was a campfire here.

Fargo settled in on the edge of the cutbank, low enough for it to act as a breastworks should he have to turn and fire quickly. The rangers had all taken up similar positions, except for Nelson. He stood nearby, his rifle in the crook of his arm, peering through the thin brush toward the north.

They remained this way for close to an hour, exchanging a few tales and waiting. Fargo's admiration for the men grew.

"Son of a bitch," Jim Nelson complained loudly.

"What's the matter?" Fargo asked.

"I tell you, Fargo, you just can't count on nothing anymore. Trust a man to lie to you an' then the son of a bitch turns around an' gets truthful when you least expect it."

"Huh?"

They were interrupted by one of the younger rangers—all of them were young, actually; Fargo doubted that Nelson had yet seen thirty—trotting over with a broad grin on his wind-burned features. "Cap'n," he said. "Donny told me to tell you that— "

"I see 'em, Bert. I see 'em." Nelson sounded pleased in spite of his complaints of a moment ago.

The young ranger called Bert turned and trotted back toward the position he had been in on their left flank.

"What was that all about?" Fargo asked. It was obvious that the Comanche were coming in, just as the rangers expected them to, but there was something . . .

Nelson grinned at him. "Like I was saying', Fargo, that damn fool lied to us. Told us a hunnert or so of the red bastards, an' we just naturally expected there to be thirty or forty o' the devils?"

"Yeah?"

"Damned if there ain't close to a hunnert of them."

A grizzled old veteran ranger of twenty-two or -three turned his head and spat a stream of yellow-brown tobacco juice into the dry creekbed, then eared back the hammer of his breech-loading Sharps. "Not more'n eighty-five, ninety at the most," he said lazily.

"Close enough," Nelson said. "That bastard as good as lied, goin' an' telling us something we couldn't possibly say was so an' then turning out t' be right. Same as a lie, anyhow."

"Lucky for us, eh, Cap'n?" the ranger said around his chew.

"Damn right, Bobby. We can really hurt them this time. Maybe keep them outta the settlements for the rest of this whole year if we whup them bad enough today."

Bobby grinned back at his captain.

This was a helluva informal outfit, Fargo had to believe. He hadn't known Jim Nelson was captain of anything until there were Comanche in sight. Certainly there were neither uniforms nor apparent military discipline in the outfit. The men dressed like a bunch of raggedy-assed cowboys and acted pretty much the same way.

Fargo yawned and stretched. He wasn't putting on a show of bravado. The yawn had nothing to do with sleepiness. It was a release of tension. He stood and picked up his own Sharps, facing the oncoming Indians and leaning against the crumbly dirt of the cutbank.

There was little enough to be seen out there, but a low swirl of dust was eddying above the mesquite a mile or so north of the creekbed. The Comanche were in a low swale now, but a moment or so earlier the rangers would have been able to see them to get a count.

Behind the men the fire continued to emit a little smoke, but less of it now. The rangers hadn't added any more greasewood to the coals after that first smoky batch of it. "Be too obvious," Nelson had explained. "Don't want them thinkin' we might have us a trap here."

Fargo looked up and down the thin line of rangers. The men were relaxed but ready. If they were worried, they managed to hide the fact damn well.

Nelson had already told him what he expected the Comanche to do. "They ain't devious," Nelson had said. "Meaner'n shit, o' course, but nothing devious about 'em. They'll come straight on in a rush. Figure they've found 'em some poor pilgrims an' figure to overwhelm 'em right off. O' course, that won't work out quite the way they figured, so the next time they'll rush our flanks. Come up the creekbed the second time. First charge, though, that'll be straightforward an' right down our throats. That's when we can hit 'em the hardest. An', Mr. Fargo, excuse me for sayin' this, but you an' me have never fought side by side. I know what my own boys will do, but . . ."

"I understand," Fargo had told the man. "No offense taken."

"Good enough, Fargo. The thing is, we like 'em to get in close enough that the wheel guns can do some work. So we'd all 'preciate it if you'd hold your fire till the rest of us cut loose. I'll shoot first. Then we can all get in on the game."

Damned if the rangers weren't treating it like a game, too. All up and down the ragged little line of rangers Fargo could see eagerness and anticipation on the lean young faces of the ranger company's boys. They were crazy—he still believed that—but they were the kind that a man could be pleased to have at his side in a scrap.

"Pretty soon now," Nelson drawled.

The boil of dust was moving closer, although the Comanche were still out of sight from this low angle. Nelson pulled a wad of cut tobacco from a pouch and shoved it into a corner of his jaw. Down the line another ranger took his pipe out of his teeth and carefully knocked the dottle out on the heel of his boot before he dropped the pipe into a pocket. The rangers cocked their rifles or carbines or shotguns and laid them onto the cutbank in front of them, then pulled their revolvers. Some of the men had one revolver in their hands and as many as four spares tucked behind their belts. Fargo palmed his own Colt and quietly checked the loads in it.

"Don't know if you've ever done this before, Mr. Fargo, but you can expect some noise when they make their charge. They figure it shakes up the enemy so bad he can't fight back worth a damn. Sometimes it does, too."

"Tell you what, then, Jim. If I piss my pants, I'll try not to get any on you."

Nelson looked at him like he thought Fargo might be serious, saw that he was not, and grinned. "Hell, Fargo, you might do."

"Thanks," he said in a dry tone.

Nelson grinned at him again, then turned his attention back to the front. The dust was damned close now, and Fargo could hear the muted thud of hundreds of pony hooves as the Comanche broke from a slow lope into a hard run for their charge on what they seemed to believe would be an unsuspecting camp of travelers.

They came into view, greasy hair and lance tips first, sweeping quickly into full sight.

They were a hell of an imposing bunch, Fargo thought: nearly naked, faces painted into hideously distorted masks, sweat or oils gleaming on their bare chests.

Most of the Comanche, though, were armed with clubs and lances and bows. Very few of them carried firearms, and many of those were awkward old flintlock trade muskets.

They must have spotted one of the Texans waiting for them, because while they were still a good fifty yards away, they broke into their screaming, ululating war cries. They sounded as fearsome as the hounds of hell, which was exactly what they intended.

The rangers calmly watched them come.

Jim Nelson stood where he was, chin high and lips pressed tight, not moving, certainly not deigning to crouch behind the natural breastworks of the cutbank, as the first arrows and flung lances arched through the air.

Forty yards. Thirty. The Comanche were screeching like madmen, working up a hell of a mad, thumping their ponies to greater speed with moccasined heels.

At twenty-five yards Nelson finally raised his revolver.

At twenty he fired, and a wave of gunsmoke spread over the line of Texans as the other rangers responded instantly with a shattering wall of lead.

Indians and ponies toppled in front of them. The rangers fired as rapidly as they could thumb their hammers and get off more shots, emptied their first revolvers, and grabbed for others.

Fargo was so interested in watching the performance of the Texans that he was slow to shoot. He made up for that with a series of quick, well-aimed shots.

A Comanche with a fingerbone necklace and a red-and-black streaked face charged toward Fargo. Fargo shot him in the chest. The Comanche screamed with hate, and Fargo shifted his sights to a very young Indian riding next to him. That one was just a kid, but he was as dangerous, as willing to kill, as any experienced warrior. Fargo's bullet thumped into his side, and the boy was reeling on his pony's back.

The dust was thick now, making it almost impossible to see for any distance except immediately to the front, and that for only a matter of yards.

The fire from the rangers was witheringly intense. The Texans weren't just shooting wildly, not just making noise, though. Fast as they were, they were cool and deliberate in their aiming.

Fargo saw a pony race across the front of the line, the horse streaming blood from a wound that had torn away one eye and half its head, its rider frantically trying to guide it but the pony too much in pain to respond to commands. Jim Nelson snapped a shot at the hapless rider, and the Comanche thumped to the ground just a few feet in front of the ranger captain, so close that Nelson had to move aside slightly to shoot around the Comanche's body.

A screaming warrior with a lance charged forward out of the swirl of dust, square onto the line of Texans. He leapt the pony over the head of the ranger called Bobby, stabbing down with his lance while the horse was in midair.

Bobby ducked under the hard hooves of the animal, and Fargo triggered a shot from the hip that struck the Comanche under the jaw and snapped what was left of the man's head almost completely around. The pony fell into the dry wash, stumbled, and rolled over. It came back onto its feet, shaking itself, and ran riderless up the creekbed, leaving the dead Comanche behind.

Another pony leapt into the wash, and another. The rangers were intent on the action to the front. No one seemed to be paying attention to the few who had gained the wash. Fargo triggered his Colt again, but the gun had run dry. He used his Sharps to blow one Comanche off his pony's back, then grabbed up the lance dropped by the Indian who had tried to kill Bobby.

The shrieking Comanche saw and wheeled his pony

toward the Trailsman. He was carrying a bow, but its string had snapped. He dropped the weapon and snatched up a war club.

They were brave bastards. Fargo certainly had to give them that.

The Trailsman stood his ground as the Comanche covered the ten or fifteen yards that separated them. The Comanche's war club was upraised and deadly. Fargo let him come in, let him commit himself to the charge, then he whipped the wicked steel tip of the lance up, jinked once to the side with it. The Indian's club swept downward to knock the lance aside. At the last instant Fargo dropped the tip and shifted it inside the sweep of the club. The tip buried itself in the Indian's chest, and the pony raced past riderless.

"Not bad," Jim Nelson said. Nelson was standing there with revolvers in both hands. He had been watching but unwilling to waste a charge unless it was needed.

"Thanks," Fargo said dryly.

"You empty?"

"Uh huh."

"Here." Nelson handed him a loaded spare and turned back to the front.

The brunt of the first charge had been broken. The live Comanches were turning back. Fargo cocked the unfamiliar revolver and shot for a spot between the shoulder blades of a Comanche who was thirty or so yards out, leaning forward over his pony's neck and urging the animal to greater speed. Instead of taking the Indian in the back as Fargo intended, the bullet raised dust and blood from the Comanche's ass. He screamed and sat upright in shocked pain. A bullet from one of the rangers found the spot where Fargo had intended to shoot and dumped the Indian onto the ground.

"Shoots a mite low," Fargo observed.

"Why d'you think I was willin' to give it away?" Nelson asked with a grin.

Fargo aimed toward the receding back of another Comanche, holding deliberately high this time. He fired but had no idea where the bullet went.

"Well, that's that," Nelson said. "At least they're nice enough to give us time to reload." His fingers were already busy stuffing fresh charges into his revolvers.

Fargo did the same. "What next?" he asked.

"They'll come again from the front, but that'll be mostly to keep us busy while a bunch of 'em come up the creek from one direction or both." The ranger captain certainly didn't sound worried about it. He was still reloading with quick, sure fingers.

Now that the dust was clearing, Fargo could see a good many dead Comanche in front of them and a good many more dead or dying horses. "I'd say you've thinned them down some."

"Ayuh. Some."

There were no wounded Comanche anywhere in sight, though, Fargo noted. All of them had either gotten away on their own or had been carried off by their companions.

"Everybody all right?" Nelson asked in a loud voice.

"Mostly," someone responded.

The kid who had given Fargo the coffee had some blood dripping off the fingers of his left hand, but he didn't seem unduly worried by his wounds. A few others had minor wounds here or there, and one man whose name Fargo didn't know had had an ear shot off but seemed otherwise unhurt. The protection of the cutbank had given them an edge.

"Aw, shit," someone complained from down the line.

"What the matter?"

"One of them bastards kicked over the coffeepot an' stomped it flat, Cap'n. Ruint it complete, they did."

"They better watch that shit," another voice said, "or they're gonna get me riled."

"Boy, if they knowed that, I'll bet they'd be scared."

Several of the rangers laughed. None of them slowed their reloading while they chattered, though.

"We got another few minutes, boys," Nelson called. "Then make sure you watch the flanks."

Fargo finished his reloading of both revolvers and the Sharps, then leaned against the cool earth of the cutbank. Before this day was out he might be glad of any rest and respite he could get.

6

"I swear," Capt. Jim Nelson complained. "Some days you just can't count on nobody to do what they ought." He reached a finger inside his mouth, hooked out his wad of chewing tobacco, examined it for a moment, and then popped it back inside his jaw. "First that Mexican as good as lyin' to us, now the damn Comanch'."

It was true enough that the Comanche were not acting as predicted. Instead of charging again and trying to break the flanks of the Texans, the Indians had drifted in afoot, armed with bows. They were lying in hiding, safe from the rangers' gunfire, forty or fifty yards out, and lofting arrows high into the air so that the deadly, sharp-tipped missiles would arch over the protective cutbank and hopefully find flesh on their way down. The arrows couldn't be aimed that way, of course, but under these circumstances chance would be as effective as deliberate action.

Already one of the men, Donny, had gotten an arrow shaft through the meat of his thigh. He had been sitting at the time. The arrow had been pulled and his wound bound, but he had to be in great pain. He was trying not to show it.

"You have something in mind?" Fargo asked.

Nelson grinned. "Yeah. I reckon we can come up with somethin'."

With this crowd of crazy Texas bastards, Fargo suspected that Jim Nelson's idea would be dangerous and difficult, but devastating.

Before Fargo could question the ranger captain, Bert came crawling over to where the two of them were sitting. "Cap'n?"

"Yeah, Bert."

"They're starting to range in on the damn horses, Cap'n. An' we got no place to hide 'em."

"Any of them down?"

"Not yet, Cap'n, but Tony's geldin' has a slice down the side of its neck, an' that brown mare o' Mr. Fargo's got pinked on the off hip."

Nelson grunted and stood. He motioned, and the rangers gathered closer so they could hear. "This sitting around waiting to be shot ain't much fun, boys," he said. "I figure it's time we took a hand in the game."

The only response from the rangers was a round of grins. They were a ready bunch.

"A bunch this size, boys, I figure they'll be traveling with a big camp. An' I figure it'd kinda discourage them some if we hit 'em there while they're out trying to raise scalps. So what I figure we oughta do is this . . ."

Nelson talked for several minutes, and the grins of the Texans got broader. When he was done speaking to his men, Nelson turned to the Trailsman. "Naturally, Fargo, you don't have to ride with us. You can break off once we get clear, if you like." He showed his teeth in a smile and spat a stream of tobacco juice. "You ain't gettin' paid all o' twenty dollars a month t' do this like all of us are."

Fargo chuckled. "I expect I can hang with you a bit longer."

"Kinda thought you'd say that, but I wanted to make

sure you knew we wouldn't think poorly of you if you wanta get on your own way now."

"That can wait a little longer."

Nelson nodded and turned back to his boys. "No point layin' around here wasting daylight, then."

The men headed for their horses, virtually ignoring the arrows that continued to drop silently into the sandy bed of the wash. They tugged their cinches tight and swung into their saddles, Fargo with them.

With a yelp that was not unlike a war cry, the rangers spurred their horses and raced with drawn revolvers down the creekbed in the direction Fargo had come from earlier in the day.

They broke past the high bank at the curve in the wash. Half a dozen Comanche were there, caught while trying to creep up on the Texans' right flank.

The Indians were afoot. All of them carried rifles or muskets, but the rangers got their shots off first. Most of the Comanche fell in that first fusillade. One of them triggered an old smooth-bore musket into the nearest ranger's side, peppering Bobby with shot and almost knocking him out of the saddle. Fargo shot the Comanche in the face as the brown mare thundered by the man. Another ranger swerved close to Bobby, steadying him in the saddle while the bunch of them raced down the wash.

Behind them they could hear angry, excited screaming as the Comanche realized that the hated Texans were getting away.

Jim Nelson whooped with glee. "That caught 'em with their pants down, boys. They left their fuckin' horses tied someplace while they came on afoot."

The rangers charged through the wash for three hundred yards or so, then found a break in the bank where they could scramble up onto the scrubby prairie.

"C'mon, boys. Let's raise us some hell."

Nelson turned his little troop north, in the direction the Comanche had come from.

Off to the left Fargo could see forty or fifty dismounted Comanche racing like hell for wherever they had left their horses.

A few of the Comanche with firearms wasted shots in the direction of the hard-riding rangers, but the slugs came nowhere near.

The rangers were riding at a belly-down run, as hard as their horses could go. The brown mare ran with them, seemingly unaffected by the slight hip wound she had received, although the unclotted scratch broke open and was showing a little blood on her right hip.

Off to Fargo's left, a good quarter of a mile away now, they could see the Comanche horse herd. The fastest Indians were nearing the horses, but most were still a good way from their horses. Fargo thought it a shame they hadn't known where the horses were being kept, or they could have run their sweep through the herd to scatter them. It was too late for that now, though, and the rangers did have a good lead over the Comanche pursuit, most of which was still taking place on foot.

Jim Nelson laughed loudly, and someone else let out a definite war whoop.

"Hot damn, boys, there they are." Nelson brandished his revolver, and the rest of his boys did the same.

Bobby was riding on his own now as the ranger who had been supporting him pulled aside and drew his revolver. The young ranger had dropped his reins over his saddle horn and was hanging on to the horn with his left hand to keep from falling off his racing horse. But he pulled his revolver and rode white-faced and determined along with the rest of them as they swept down toward the Comanche encampment they could now see a hundred fifty yards ahead.

No tepees had been erected at the Comanche camp yet, but the pack horses had been unloaded and cooking pots suspended on wooden tripods over small fires.

There were some women among the Indians in camp,

Fargo could see, and probably a dozen wounded men already brought back there to be tended. The Comanche saw the charging Texans. The women scattered for the scant, scrubby brush, and those wounded who could do so were trying to struggle to their feet and reach for weapons. The Comanche horse herd—there were far too many of them to all be pack animals, so apparently the raiders traveled with a good supply of loose stock— was beyond the temporary camp.

Fargo could see Nelson's intentions clearly as the ranger captain altered direction by a few degrees. The rangers intended to make a quick strike through the camp and then scatter the horses.

Most of the Texans set up a sharp, yipping cry as they closed on the camp. The sound of their racing horses' hooves was like thunder in the late-afternoon air.

Nelson reached the camp first. He jumped his horse over the body of a wounded Comanche, shooting down into the man's chest as he leapt over the buffalo-robe bed.

The rangers hauled their horses down to a dust-raising stop and wheeled about, revolvers spitting lead at anything that moved and at a fair number of things that didn't.

Most of the rangers had emptied their first revolvers and were well on their way to working through their second cylinders before Fargo fired his first round. Shooting women—even Comanche women who would be delighted to raise his hair and torture him to death afterward—was not something he found comfortable.

A mounted Comanche came rushing in from some-where near. The Indian loosed an arrow in the general direction of the milling, shooting Texans before Fargo put a bullet into his belly. The man toppled to the ground, and Donny, ignoring the wound in his thigh, rode over the man and finished him with a bullet in the back of his skull.

"Go!" Nelson shouted, and the Texans spurred their excited horses toward the Comanche herd.

The brown mare balked for just a moment, lagging behind the others. Fargo snatched at the bit to get her attention and spurred her after the others. Getting left behind in this camp probably wouldn't be a good idea today.

Finally the brown jumped forward.

But Fargo yanked her to a halt again. Behind him he could hear a distinctly unhappy cry of "Oh, shit!"

It was Bobby. He was down, his horse racing off after the other rangers without him. He lay flat, his revolver still in his hand and his entire left shoulder and side soaked with scarlet blood from where the Comanche back in the wash had shot him with the old smooth-bore.

Fargo wheeled the brown back toward Bobby and bent low. "Grab hold," he shouted.

Bobby raised his right hand, dropping his revolver as he did so, and grabbed frantically for Fargo's wrist as the brown raced past him.

He was virtually deadweight, nearly pulling both of them down as Fargo levered him awkwardly up. With his one good hand Bobby clutched the far side of Fargo's saddle, draping himself over the brown's rump and clinging there tight as a tick while once again Fargo spun the horse in the direction the rangers had gone.

To the south there were mounted Comanche approaching. They were every bit as furious as Fargo would have expected them to be, and some of them were already flinging long-range shots toward the two men on the brown horse.

"Let's . . ."

A Comanche rolled into sight, a heavy-caliber horse pistol leveled. Fargo swung his Colt and fired, sending a bullet into the Comanche's chest even before he saw it was a young and not unattractive woman he had just shot.

79

A woman, though, who had been intent on killing him, dammit.

There was no help for that now. He spurred the brown forward.

Up ahead Nelson and the other rangers had noticed the absence of Fargo and Bobby. Half of them stopped, ready to give covering fire until Fargo could catch up to them, while the rest rode shooting and whooping through the Indian horse herd.

The horses bolted in all directions, and several of them were brought down by the Texans' gunfire.

Nelson stood coolly in his stirrups, a rifle in his hands now. He took careful aim and dropped the nearest Comanche. "Let's go, dammit," the ranger captain called.

Immediately the troop wheeled and pounded off toward the north, several of them dropping back to help cover Fargo and their wounded companion.

"Hot damn," someone shouted. "Dark soon. They won't be chasin' much tonight. We got to 'em this time, boys."

"Reload boys," Jim Nelson called. "Don't get lazy now."

The little troop of rangers thundered off toward the northern horizon.

The meat was good. Dripping with grease and barely on the fire long enough to char on the outside, it was definitely good and most definitely welcome. One of the boys had shot a pair of javelinas in the brush in the last light of the dusk, and the ranger troop hadn't hesitated to build a fire to roast the fresh meat. Now most of them were bitching because that Comanche pony had stepped on their only coffeepot and left it flat as a johnnycake.

Skye Fargo still thought they were a crazy bunch of bastards, but they sure as hell could fight.

They took care of their own, too. They had Bobby propped on the seat of his saddle and were feeding him choice bits of the strength-giving meat. They had already cleaned up his arm and shoulder as well as they were able. That part of their treatment of him had brought more laughter than sympathy, though. The Comanche had shot him with a load of small pebbles that had been stuffed down the barrel of the flint musket.

Now the rangers were all sitting around the campfire like they hadn't a care in the world.

"What next, Jim?" Fargo asked.

"Aw, come tomorra, we'll take a look-see at those Comanch' again. If they're headed back for the damn Llano we'll hurry them along, I reckon. Otherwise"—he grinned—"we'll hafta see can we set 'em up for another little go-round like today's."

Fargo looked skeptically toward the wounded men. Bobby was in bad shape, although with luck he might be able to keep his arm and eventually return to active service. Donny's thigh was bad too.

"Hell, Skye"—they had gotten onto a first-name basis after Fargo went back to rescue the downed ranger—"six is plenty. Seven if you wanta come along, o' course. You're sure welcome to join us."

One of the boys sitting next to Nelson leaned over and whispered something to the captain.

"Just leave be, dammit. I already thought o' that. I'm gettin' to it."

"Well, all right, then."

Nelson grinned at Fargo. "You got yourself a vote o' confidence, Trailsman. The boys say they'd be willin' to see you sign on as a ranger yourself. Draw wages an' everything. Twenty a month an' found. You supply your own horse an' weapons. We buy your ammunition."

"I'm flattered," Fargo said. He meant it. Nothing was said, exactly, but he suspected that an invitation to join this wild bunch was rare and should be considered something of an honor. On the other hand, he had fish to fry that had nothing to do with chasing tribes of wild Comanche back to the Llano Estacado. "But I'm out here for a reason, boys. If it wasn't for that, I'd be proud to join you. As it is, I'd best head my own way, come morning."

He couldn't help remembering that the gang and his own Ovaro had pulled that much more of a lead on him while he was occupied playing games with the ranger detachment this afternoon. "I wish I could do it."

Nelson nodded. Fargo was pleased to see that several of the boys looked actually disappointed that he wouldn't be joining them permanently.

Fargo noticed, too, that none of them pressed him for explanations or tried to talk him out of his decision. If he said he had business, he had business. They were too polite to inquire about what that business might be.

Nelson turned to Donny. "I don't know which way Skye will be ridin' tomorra, but if it's back toward the settlements, you an' Bobby might wanta ride along with him for comp'ny."

"Bobby could," Donny said. "That'd be a big help. I'm fit to go on with you, though, Cap'n."

"I said with you an' Bobby. I meant with you an' Bobby," Jim Nelson said softly.

The captain's voice had been mild as rainwater, but Donny reacted like he'd just been chewed out by a top sergeant. He cut his eyes away from Nelson's and looked down toward his boot toes with misery written all over him.

He didn't argue it any further, though, Fargo noticed, and didn't complain. Apparently it was not that discipline in this outfit was lacking, just that it wasn't out where strangers might stare at it. Jim Nelson was a most efficient leader of men.

"I haven't had a chance before to ask," Fargo said, "but have you boys seen anything of six men riding west?" He described them for the rangers, particularly the Ovaro that he sought.

Nelson looked at him closely. "I didn't think you'd be riding with that crowd, Skye." He didn't exactly ask what Fargo wanted with them. But it was clear that he wanted to.

"Not hardly," Fargo said. He explained why he wanted to know.

"Shit," a ranger named Jarvis said. "I knew there was something funny about them."

"You did see them, then?"

"Ayuh," Nelson confirmed. "Last evenin'. Headed west, all right, just like you said. Damn! If we'd knowed about that bank, we coulda saved you a lot o' trouble. Us too if you happen to miss 'em and the job comes to us."

"We invited them to come along and shoot some Comanch'," Jarvis said, "but they wasn't interested."

"Huh. No wonder," Bert put in. "Cain't you just see a bunch of assholes like that pitching in with the best damn comp'ny of rangers on the frontier? Shee-it. But I sure wisht we'd known. We coulda been on them boys like stink on shit. Damn pity we didn't know."

"If you run into them again, you'll know," Fargo said.

"Damn straight we would."

"If that happens, Skye, though I wouldn't say it's likely, you can be sure you'll get your horse back."

"I'll tend to him myself," the kid offered.

Fargo thanked him. This was one good bunch of boys.

"If you're riding after that bunch," Nelson said, "I expect you'll be going alone. My boys got to go the other direction. Nearest doc is a hundred fifty miles or so."

Donny looked like he wanted to protest again, but he kept quiet.

"Sorry it doesn't work out that way. Did those men say where they were headed?"

Nelson grinned. "Uh huh. Talked loud an' clear about El Paso del Nort'. Which means, if I figure 'em correctly, that's just about the last place you'd wanta look for them. Unless there's something you know that we don't."

Fargo shook his head. "West. That's about all I've got figured so far. Just west."

"Santa Fe might be likely. Or one of them Mexican settlements over in that country. O' course, that's way the hell an' gone the other side of the Llano. Bad country between there an' here, Skye. You'll want to ride careful."

"What about water?" Fargo asked. "I've heard that can be seldom."

"You heard right, then. We oughta be having rains this time o' year, but they haven't come yet. Some years they never do. You have canteens?"

"That one hanging on my saddle."

Nelson nodded toward the kid, and the youngster went and fetched the two canteens owned by the two wounded rangers.

"You can have these. The boys ain't going anywhere that they'll need 'em soon. They can replace 'em when they get to town." He turned toward Donny. "Charge the replacements t' the battalion. I'll square it with the major when we get back."

Donny nodded.

"I don't know how to thank you boys for the help. That much more water could mean a difference to me."

Jim Nelson looked down toward Bobby, who had either gone to sleep or quietly passed out during the last few minutes. "Might be one ranger fewer if you hadn't helped him out this afternoon. I expect this is the least we can do. We'd be pleased t' go with you after those boys if we didn't have to keep those damn Comanch' off the settlements."

"That's more important," Fargo said. "I'm just sorry I can't ride with you any farther."

"If there's anything any Texas Ranger can do for you, Trailsman, you just tell 'im Jim Nelson an' his boys say

84

it's owed. He'll give you the hand or answer to us for not."

The man meant it too, and so did his young troopers. Fargo really did regret that he couldn't ride farther with them. They were quite a crowd.

Fargo rode west a good many miles before he swung south again to pick up the gang's trail. He had no desire to run into that Comanche war party again, particularly while he was riding alone. It had been touchy enough with the rangers beside him. One man alone would have no chance except in flight.

At least the damned mare seemed to be in good shape. She had come close to dumping him this morning while she worked the kinks out of her spine. The grazing cut she had received from a Comanche arrow seemed to have done no real damage, and before Fargo left, the young kid insisted on painting the cut with a mixture of turpentine and resin. The medication made an ugly blotch on the mare's hide, but then the horse was ugly to begin with. Fargo wanted her for her toughness and the hell with how bedraggled she looked. If it was pretty he was after, he probably would have shot the horse and ridden a burro instead.

He crossed the Comanche line of march about midmorning. The six robbers had been damned lucky. The war party had to have crossed the robbers' tracks yesterday. By then, though, the Indians must have been intent on the smoke they could see ahead of them and either missed spotting the tracks left behind by the horsemen, or ignored them in favor of the nearer target represented by that smoke.

Lucky, indeed, Fargo thought. Trying to retrieve the black-and-white pinto from a Comanche horse herd wouldn't be high on his list of want-to's.

He rode on, through country that became ever drier the farther west he went, swinging south finally.

It was slow going for a while then. He hadn't seen

the gang's hoofprints since roughly midday yesterday, and he didn't want to blindly assume that they would continue their westwardly course. Time-consuming though it was to find the expertly hidden trail, he had to do it. To make an error now could cost him days, even weeks, of futile travel.

He began to wish that he had taken more time with Jane. Perhaps he could have gotten her to tell him where the gang was going if he had really pushed her on the issue. Too late for that now, of course.

Thinking about Jane had been a mistake. She had been out of his thoughts practically from the moment he left her. Now . . .

He rode west with the sun hard and hot on his shoulders and an erection hard and hot inside his fly. Damn the girl anyhow.

The saddle he had gotten with the brown was shorter in the seat than his own comfortable rig. The smooth, swift road jog of the brown mare rocked him back and forth lightly, shoving his pecker up and down against the back of the horn stem on the short saddletree. Now that he'd got to thinking about Jane, dammit, that was becoming a problem.

The problem disappeared abruptly when the Trails-man's attention was drawn to something of much more immediate interest.

A mile or so ahead and off to Fargo's left he could see a black-winged carrion-eater wheeling in the sky. Then more of them became apparent as his attention was placed on that quarter. While he watched, several of the huge birds spiraled lower in the sky until they disappeared from view against the rugged, broken terrain of west Texas.

Fargo grimaced. Vultures, buzzards, magpies . . . they were the celebrants of death. Wherever a man rode, there was always one of them near, eager to pick his bones and feast on his flesh if only he would be accommodating enough to die.

Still, they would as eagerly descend on a dead jackrabbit as a dead Jack or Robert. It was entirely possible, even likely, that their presence in front of him now had nothing to do with human violence.

Either way, he wanted to know.

Fargo twitched the leather of his reins against the brown's neck, altering her course slightly to take him toward the spot where the huge birds continued to gather and to swoop low in the sky.

A dead coyote, he told himself. A dying javelina. With luck, that would be all he would find there.

But he had to know.

There were coyotes when he rode up, but no dead ones. Two of the scruffy gray bastards slunk off into the brush. They had been feeding on something that used to be human.

Fargo dismounted and tied the brown to a wheel on one of the abandoned wagons that had been raided.

It was a hell of a mess that had been left behind.

There were only two wagons. No livestock, draft or saddle, in sight.

There were some bodies, however.

What with the coyotes and vultures and who knew what else overnight, the bodies weren't pretty to look at.

The wagons had been coming up from the southeast, heading toward Horsehead Crossing over to New Mexico or maybe pointed toward Raton or Pueblo way the hell and gone to the north. Movers, Fargo guessed, given up on Texas and bent on trying yet another, more distantly westward location.

Their moving was ended now.

The wagons had been thoroughly ransacked. There was no way he could tell exactly what they had been carrying, but some things were obvious and it was possible to guess at others.

The food boxes had been rifled. Everything not taken had been ruined. Coal oil poured into the cornmeal.

Bacon crate broken and thrown onto the ground; it was empty now after the night's visitations by predators and scavengers. Salt scattered on the ground. A crumpled Arbuckle's bag emptied of the coffee and tossed aside.

That much Fargo could almost understand. That and the gaping, shattered wood of the false wagon bottom where the people must have kept their cash.

Thievery he could at least understand.

Wanton destruction he could not.

A handsome mirror on a beautifully carved oak stand had been thrown out of one wagon and destroyed. Quicksilvered shards of old, brittle glass lay on the ground there.

Trunks had been thrown open, and their contents of clothing—some rather fine at one time but outdated by current fashion now—ripped and torn before they were thrown into the dirt.

Damn the kind of man who would do this, Fargo thought. Damn each of them.

At first he had assumed that the terror and the destruction had been at the hands of a scouting party of the Comanche.

One look at the ground beneath his feet disproved that.

The hoofprints of the Ovaro were there.

Fargo felt a cold, tight knot deep in his gut at the knowledge.

He had been deliberately avoiding the bodies. But there was no way around it.

The Comanche would have done no worse by these poor people than the six whites had done. Probably they would have done less. At least, if the Comanche had attacked, the movers would have had some warning. They would have known to go for their rifles as soon as a band of Comanche came into sight.

Not so with the whites. The tracks left on the sun-baked soil told that tale clear. The two parties, gang and movers, had approached each other at an angle.

Neither party hurried. The gang had probably hailed the wagons as friendly passersby and had approached them at a slow, easy walk, likely smiling and waving, calling howdies back and forth. Where you from? Where you bound?

When they were close enough, perhaps after they had been invited to stop and share a meal or a pot of coffee, the gang cut down on unsuspecting, unarmed men. And at least one woman.

Jesus! Fargo thought.

The bodies weren't easy to identify, so badly had they been ravaged. One very old man. Two mature men. One half-grown boy. One middle-aged woman.

Fargo felt himself go colder as he thought of something. He went back to the nearer of the wagons to check on something.

He had no clear idea of exactly how many innocent people had been in those two wagons. The soil was too hard and the tracks too thoroughly disturbed by much coming and going for him to be sure of that. But there was clothing in the one wagon that would indicate at least one more adult woman in the party.

Fargo looked farther afield, hunting in widening circles around the death scene, but there were no other bodies in the area.

If there had been other females with the wagons, the gang had carried them along.

Those bastards were building themselves quite a party, Fargo thought. First the horses stolen from Norman Walters. Now horses and probably women taken from these wagons.

Those men were developing quite a debt.

It was a debt they were going to have to pay soon.

Skye Fargo figured to call in those markers if it was the last thing he had breath to do.

No, he amended. Not quite the last. In addition to these men, there was another group he also had to find before he died. That was a debt that was even greater.

He took another look at the murdered family lying dead and abused on the hard prairie.

No. Not a greater debt. Not, at least, so far as any survivors of this unfortunate family would be concerned.

A different debt, then. One more immediately personal to the man who now called himself Skye Fargo.

The debt itself would be very much the same. Ugly, soulless, vile men who took for themselves and left behind blood and pain and the awful, utter destruction of a family.

Fargo shuddered and felt his gut churn with bile as he rummaged through the wagons until he found a spade, its handle broken for no purpose except for sheer destruction, and began to dig a grave to receive the bodies of the murdered folk.

When he paused in the digging, his eyes searched off toward the west, in the direction the murderers had gone.

The look in those lake-blue eyes was as cold as the inside of Fargo's heart when he thought about the six men.

And about the accounting he intended to bring to them.

7

The murderers were moving slowly indeed now, with all the extra baggage and booty they were taking along with them.

Fargo found their night camp before he had been on the trail more than a few hours the next morning. They were, he judged, not more than a dozen miles ahead of him, and moving much slower than he was able to.

A grim expression that might have been mistaken for a smile thinned and tightened Fargo's lips.

Today. He would catch up with them today. He was sure of it. Fargo grunted with satisfaction.

Then the satisfied expression disappeared as a puff of breeze carried an unexpected scent to him.

The odor was that of decaying flesh. For a moment he couldn't identify it.

Then, with a knot lying heavy in his belly like frozen lead, already half-sure of what he would find, he moved into the low brush around the gang's campsite to investigate.

He found very much what he expected to find: there was a body dumped unheeded and unburied into the low-growing brush.

It was a man Fargo recognized. The Trailsman had last seen the man on a San Antonio street. At the time the son of a bitch had been mounted on the black-and-white Ovaro, and Fargo had put a bullet into him.

That bullet had finally done its work.

The man's shirt had been removed and he had been crudely bandaged. Some time before the robber's death the bandage had been pulled apart to expose the wound Fargo had put there. The flesh around the wound had festered, the greasy, powder-fouled lead of the slug had been dirty enough to begin with and likely had carried scraps of cloth and sweat and who knew what else into the torn flesh when it entered. Without proper care from the robber's companions, the wound had become infected, streaks of dark red surrounding it, reaching farther into the living body of the wounded man, until green-gray gangrene spread from the wound into the body.

After that, death was inevitable.

But the other five gang members hadn't waited for their partner to slowly die in screaming agony, slowing them in the meantime and possibly giving them away to wandering Indians by shrieking at the wrong time.

Some time last night they—or someone—had helped the fellow along into the death that had to come to him soon.

The man had been knifed to death, a stab wound low in the belly, a rough way to die even for a man already racked with gangrene.

Fargo examined the body briefly. Then he took a look around the place where the gang had camped.

The dead man was dressed except for his shirt, and that had been wadded into a blood-crusted ball and discarded in the brush near the ashes of the gang's campfire.

He stopped. Caught in the brush was a wad of long, very long brown hair.

At least one woman had been captured from the wagons, then. He had suspected it before. So the murderous bastards had a hostage with them.

Fargo grunted into the stillness of the midmorning air. Not a hostage, he amended. A plaything for the gang members.

He looked off toward the west, his eyes cold and jaw hard set. The Trailsman mounted the brown mare and left the body unburied behind him as he resumed the trail the gang had left behind when they broke camp this morning.

Somewhere up ahead—not too very many miles ahead now—there was a living woman who needed help.

And Skye Fargo didn't figure to be a minute longer reaching those sons of bitches now than was absolutely necessary.

He booted the tough brown mare into a lope and set off in pursuit of the gang.

He saw the dust they were raising before he ever saw the horses and riders. That many animals, their own plus the stock they had stolen, would raise a cloud behind them no matter how carefully they were moving. And, in fact, the gang seemed to have abandoned all thought of pursuit and now were riding along like they hadn't a care in the world.

Wrong. Fargo's eyes narrowed. But then their inattention was all to the good now.

Still, they were stupid sons of bitches about that, no matter how bloodily efficient they might be in a bank building or raiding some isolated homestead or wagon train. Anywhere in this unsettled country there was always the danger of Comanches or Kiowas.

A Comanche scout could spot rising dust quite as easily as the Trailsman could. Fargo had no illusions about that. And he already knew for certain that there was a raiding party on the move right now—probably a hundred miles or more away by now but certainly on the move. And no sensible man would count knowing for sure where that or any other body of Comanche raiders would be at any given moment unless he was looking directly at them.

The gang wasn't being bright about their travel.

But that was all to the good for Fargo's purposes.

He glanced toward the sky. The sun was barely on the downside of its zenith. Call it two o'clock, give or take a bit. The remaining five gang members and their plaything must have stopped to cook dinner. Fargo had continued in the saddle, allowing the brown only the rest of dropping from a lope into a jog while he ate some of Jane's honey-nut mixture for his lunch.

So far so good.

It never occurred to him that he might question the advisability of one man taking on five armed murderers. Odds were not at issue here. Retrieving the Ovaro was. And exacting repayment for the debts those men piled up behind them.

He eased the brown back into a jog again and stood in his stirrups to get a better look at the terrain ahead.

The horse's slower speed was still fast enough to let him close on the slow-moving group ahead and slightly to the right of him.

What he wanted was a place where he might be able to swing around the gang and take a good position ahead of them. Get them coming in. Intercept them and use the Sharps to cut down on them before they knew he was there. Shorten the odds and then close on them with his revolvers. He had the firepower of his own Colt plus the low-shooting .44 Walker that Jim Nelson had given him.

Hell, with that much firepower available he could kill each of the sons of bitches twice. He smiled grimly at the thought. It would have pleased him to be able to do exactly that.

The thin swirl of dust showed that the men were riding steadily westward now, straight as a string.

Far off toward the horizon Fargo could see some low, rugged buttes. Nearer there were no significant features except the unending, dry, flat spread of the west Texas scrub.

He didn't want to wait until the gang reached those buttes. For one thing, they were too far away, eight or ten miles.

More important, the gang could well be heading for some specific place for their night stop at or near those gray, rocky humps in the earth. There could be—probably was—a water tank somewhere near the base of one of them. Fargo could set his ambush only to have the gang angle off at the last moment toward some other specific destination. He didn't want to chance that.

The easy thing to do would be to wait. Hang back and watch from afar until they made their night camp and then jump them from the darkness.

The problem with that would be that it would give the bastards opportunity to take another crack at the woman, or women, they still had with them.

Whoever that poor woman was, she didn't deserve that. Not if Fargo could do anything about it. She had already suffered quite enough.

He rejected the idea of waiting that long and swerved the brown to a low rise that was slightly higher than the flat land around it.

There was nothing ahead that looked like a good spot for an ambush. No washes that he could see. No swales he might follow. Certainly no gaps or arroyos that the gang would be forced to take. In this barren, ugly land a man could run a horse flat out for the better part of a day and rarely have to worry about obstacles any more serious than an occasional prairie-dog hole.

Fargo eased back into his saddle with a frown.

He wanted those men. He damn well intended to take them. Now.

He pulled Jim Nelson's revolver out of his saddlebags and shoved it behind his belt, then slid the stubby Sharps out of its boot and laid it across his pommel.

He kicked the brown into a loose, swift lope and headed straight at the sons of bitches.

"Howdy. Howdy, boys. Wait for me, will you?" Fargo rode up behind the gang like a passing traveler eager for company and the protection of others, shouting and waving and trying to look as friendly and innocent as he could.

That, after all, was how the bastards must have approached the now dead travelers in those wagons. It was a trick that could have a sting on both sides.

"Wait for me, boys," he called loudly as he came within hearing of the men.

He rode easy, balancing the Sharps carbine with his rein hand and waving wildly with his right.

There were five of the sons of bitches, the smallest of them riding the powerful Ovaro. The Ovaro was right there, not a hundred yards off now, in the hands of a damn thief and murderer. Fargo tried not to think about that now, though, because there was a sixth figure riding with them. A short, thin-bodied female with her skirts enveloping the saddle of the crow-bait horse she was riding. As much as Fargo thought of his horse, the woman was more important right now.

He smiled and waved and shouted again, and the riders moved into a tighter bunch to talk over his presence before they responded.

He knew damn good and well what they would do. They could be expected to greet him warmly . . . and then to kill him the very first chance they got. This crowd was willing to kill anyone they ran across and to steal whatever they could get their hands on. There would be nothing in the appearance of one more lone traveler to change that.

Actually, they were doing pretty well for themselves so far. They had left San Antonio with six horses and six riders. They were down to five men now, but they were driving a good twenty head of loose stock with them. And, of course, they had the woman captive to play with during the long evenings, plus whatever else they might have stolen along the way. Two of the loose horses were carrying packs, probably with food and valuables taken from the Walters place and from the two wagons.

The bastards probably thought they were in tall cotton. And now here was another victim coming along and asking them to slow down so they could rob and kill him too.

What more could miserable shits like that want? It would be almost too good to be true.

Much too good to be true, Fargo conceded. But he continued to smile and wave to the pricks.

The five men conferred briefly, then two of them dropped back to meet him. The other three and the woman continued.

Fargo noticed that two of those three moved so that they were flanking the woman, and one of them leaned over and spoke to her. Probably they were warning her to do nothing that would alarm their next victim.

The false smile was wiped away from Fargo's tanned face and was replaced by a look of dark determination.

This pigeon wasn't going to be so easy to pluck.

"Howdy," one of the men said as the two riders came near. He was smiling. With every bit as much sincerity as Fargo. "If you're goin' west, friend, you should ride along with us. We'll all be safer from the stinkin' redskins that way."

"That's just what I was thinking," Fargo told him. "Safer for everybody if we get together." He smiled.

Sincerely this time. Hell, he was telling the exact truth there. It would be safer for everybody in Texas once they did get together. Except, that is, for five certain assholes who liked to murder and steal. And the way Skye Fargo saw it, those five didn't count anyhow.

"My name's Berry," the asshole said. He grinned. "Everybody calls me Razz, an' I expect you can too."

The other man didn't speak but hung back a few yards while Berry rode close and turned his horse so that he was riding beside Fargo.

Fargo had an idea of what might be coming. Before Berry could speak, Fargo said, "No need to be riding so scared now. Let me put this thing away." He shoved his carbine back into its boot under his leg.

Berry nodded and grinned, happy that the victim was cooperating so nicely and was so completely unsuspecting. He reined a little nearer the brown mare and held his hand out for Fargo to shake. "What's your name, neighbor?"

Fargo told him, and with a smile accepted the handshake.

Still grinning, Berry tightened his grip on Skye Fargo's gun hand, clamping with surprising power so that he held Fargo like a vise. He pulled, yanking Fargo off balance in the saddle, and shouted, "I got 'im, Lew."

Berry's quiet partner grabbed for Fargo's revolver while Razz Berry continued to immobilize Skye's gun hand.

They expected him to panic. They expected him to be confused. They expected him to be shot down in cold blood with a .44-caliber slug through his belly. It was much like a pair of bullies outside a schoolhouse: You hold him, Razz, and I'll hit him.

Except that Skye Fargo wasn't the cooperative type. Not like that, he wasn't.

Fargo squeezed back on Berry's hand, damn near crushing the man's fingers in his iron grip, while with his free hand he hauled out Jim Nelson's revolver from behind his belt and shot the second man in the face.

At such close range he hadn't had to worry so much about the gun throwing low, he saw.

Fargo had aimed deliberately high, and the marble-sized bullet crushed through the bridge of the murderer's nose, carrying flesh and cartilage with it deep into the gray mush that had been the man's brain.

Not that the murderer cared. By then he was beyond giving a damn about anything.

Razz Berry went suddenly pale and tried to pull his own gun hand free so he could go for the revolver that rode at his left hip.

But now the trap had been reversed. Now it was the Trailsman who was holding him pinioned.

"Jesus, mister . . ." Berry hesitated.

"Good thinking," Fargo said calmly. "Maybe He'll help you. I sure won't." He tipped the muzzle of the Colt Walker toward Berry's gut and cocked the massive weapon.

The big Walker was the same caliber as Fargo's own .44, but its huge cylinder carried a powder charge half again as heavy as in the more common modern weapon.

Berry looked into the gaping muzzle of the old Walker and went pale. He sucked his gut in involuntarily, trying to steel it against the impact of the expected bullet.

Apparently killing was just fine when it was done to others. Not so damn much fun when he himself was about to go under.

"What . . .?" Apparently it had occurred to Berry that Fargo had not yet shot him. But he was so frightened and so confused by now that he couldn't get the question out of his constricted throat.

"Want to live, do you?"

Berry gulped and nodded. "Jesus! Yes!"

"Anything could happen," Fargo said, which was not

exactly a lie. Strange things might always be possible. "Get your pals to turn the girl loose and come back here. We'll have it out, Razz. You an' them against me, Razz. But eyeball to eyeball. Not quite so easy as the murders you've been doing lately, eh?"

"Jesus, mister, I . . ." Berry was so pale he looked like he was going to faint dead away and fall out of his saddle.

A hundred fifty yards ahead, the rest of the gang had come to a stop. They had been expecting to hear gunshots, of course, but now one of them had noticed that it was the wrong man—at least from their point of view—who'd gotten shot.

The three men were staring back toward Fargo and Berry and the dead gang member. One of them spun his horse back in that direction, but the little man on the Ovaro said something and the fellow hauled his horse to a stop again.

"They don't seem to be rushing to your rescue, Razz," Fargo observed.

"Jesus, mister . . ."

"I do wish you'd quit saying that. Seems sacrilegious coming from an asshole like you."

"Yessir," Berry said quickly.

"No, Razz, I don't think they're coming back for you at all. See? They're turning away from their old buddy Razz. Going to run while they can, Razz. Of course, there's no place they can run that I won't find them. But they don't know that, do they?"

"Look, mister, Jeez . . . I mean, uh, I know . . . if you want Calder an' them, I can help you. You know? I could be a big help to you. Really."

The three gang members were spurring their horses into a run now, ignoring the stolen herd of loose stock but dragging the woman's horse with them.

Fargo's lips tightened.

He was *not* going to let them get away from him now.

He still was clinging to Razz Berry's sweaty hand. The asshole had sweat so much in his panic that he probably could have pulled free of Fargo's grip now if he tried, but he was so thoroughly cowed that he wasn't even making a token resistance.

Fargo glanced toward the murderous son of a bitch who seemed so docile now but who could be absolutely counted on to put a bullet into Fargo's back if he got half a second of opportunity.

Without debate or concern about it, Fargo squeezed the trigger of the huge Walker and sent a slug low into the belly of the murderer, turning loose the man's hand while he did so.

Berry was flung out of his saddle by the impact. His horse sidestepped nervously, then became panicked by the dead thing that was hanging off the saddle with one boot twisted and trapped into the stylish oxbow stirrup. The horse tried to kick free of the blood-smelly object, then bolted into a run, Berry's body flopping and dragging beside it.

But by then Fargo was no longer watching. He was spurring forward in pursuit of the remaining three gang members.

The four riders had less than two hundred yards on him, and the brown mare was a fast horse—not as quick as the Ovaro but certainly better than any of the rest of them.

Within moments Fargo burst through the crowd of loose and now thoroughly confused stolen stock, the pack horses among them, and raced on after the spurring, quirting gang. The loose horses whinnied and threw their heads, then broke into a run behind Fargo, their herd instinct impelling them to run with the saddled horses.

Up ahead, one of the men turned in his saddle and threw a hurried shot in Fargo's direction. It was a futile attempt, the bullet coming nowhere near. Fargo stood in his stirrups, the big Walker still in his hand. There was no point in shooting now, though. The range was impossibly long for a handgun and would have been just as doubtful with a rifle because of the movement of the running horse. The man who said he could shoot with any degree of accuracy from the back of a running horse was a liar.

Quickly the little man on the Ovaro took a lead over his companions. Calder, Fargo assumed. If he was the one who had taken over the Ovaro, he almost had to be the leader of the gang, the one Berry had spoken of. Fargo wanted all of them. But this Calder first and foremost.

The other two lashed their horses with their rein ends and raked the animals with their spur rowels, but the beasts had only so much to give. And Fargo was closing on them now. The brown was pulling nearer with every bunch and thrust of her long, powerful haunches.

He drew within a hundred fifty yards of them. A hundred. Seventy-five.

Again one of them tried a shot at him, but again the slug didn't come near enough for him to even hear. The man was wasting powder. He was welcome to do all of that he wished. Fargo leaned forward over the mare's neck, balancing on his toes to put as much of his weight as possible over her withers, where it wouldn't impede her.

One of the men shouted something to the other across the back of the crow-bait horse the woman was on.

That inferior animal was holding them back, pulling constantly on its lead rope and dragging behind the horse of the murderer who was leading it like an anchor turned loose in the sea.

The gunman shouted something to his partner, then turned and fired off two, three, four quick shots toward Fargo. One was close enough for him to hear the high-pitched, snarling buzz of its passage, but it did no harm. The man dropped his empty revolver into his holster and pulled another gun from a holster strapped to his saddle.

Fargo was tempted, but he held his fire. His concentration was wholly on riding down those killers. First these two. Then Calder, who by now was three hundred yards or more out front on the big pinto and pulling farther away.

Damn the man anyhow, Fargo thought bitterly.

But Calder's time was coming. First Fargo had these others to deal with.

The man who was leading the woman's sluggish horse dragged his rein a little, slowing his mount and letting the led horse catch up. He shouted something to his companion, and the second man nodded.

The first one took out his pistol and whipped the barrel across the face of the woman.

She screamed and fell backward, dropping out of her saddle like a sack of grain dropped off the tailgate of a moving wagon.

Immediately the son of a bitch released the lead rope of her horse and let the quickly tiring animal drop away while the two murderers spurred forward.

Fargo thundered down on the crying, bleeding woman, who had rolled over and over with the speed of her fall to end up sprawled in a clump of prickly pear.

Bastards!

The three were so close now.

Almost within pistol range.

But, dammit . . .

Cursing inwardly, Fargo reined the mare to a dancing, nervous halt over the now-still form of the woman.

The horse wheeled and curvetted, eager to be back in the chase. The ugly bitch wasn't good for much, but she seemed to like a race. Even a race to the death. Speed was what she was built for, and Fargo was taking that away from her.

He shoved the Colt back behind his belt and snatched at the Sharps, swinging it to his shoulder in a swift, fluid motion, thumbing back the hammer, rising in his stirrups to aim.

He settled the blade of the front sight squarely between the shoulders of the retreating gunman on the left and squeezed off his shot.

The damn mare moved and fidgeted just as he touched off the trigger, and his bullet went wide, striking the earth far beyond the two horsemen and between them.

"Dammit," Fargo muttered out loud. He was enraged enough to take after them again.

But then the woman groaned, the sound low and piteous, and weakly tried to roll away from the sharp thorns of the prickly pear.

She hadn't the strength to move that far and slumped back onto the soft, pulpy tunas.

"Dammit," Fargo groaned again, but in frustration this time. He couldn't leave her alone here, hurt, maybe near to dying. There was no telling what these sons of bitches would have done to her. He couldn't ride on after them—not until he had at least seen to her, seen if there was anything he could do to help.

That was exactly what the bastards would be hoping for, of course. They would be counting on that kind of "weakness" in his character that would make it impossible for him to abandon an injured woman and continue the chase.

There was no help for it, though. He had to watch them recede into the distance while he sat helpless to do anything about their escape.

Helpless right now, Fargo thought. But only for right now. As soon as he had seen to the woman . . .

He reloaded, then dropped the Sharps back into its scabbard and dismounted. There was nothing sturdy to which he could tie the brown, so he took additional time to hobble the horse, then went to the woman.

Already the other horses, both pack animals and the loose stock, had dropped from hard runs into a trot and were coming closer, gathering to the man who meant security and some degree of comfort to them.

Fargo knelt beside the woman and touched her on the shoulder. "Ma'am?" he said softly.

There was no response. She seemed to have passed out.

Fargo eased her away from the prickly pear and rolled her onto her back, moving her as gently and easily as he could so as to cause her no more additional pain than was necessary.

He gasped when he saw her, and his eyes tightened, lifting involuntarily toward the west and the now-distant, unseen murderers.

The pistol-whipping had hit her across the mouth, so that the front of her face was bloody and several teeth were gone. In addition to that, she had a haggard, unhealthy look about her. There were dark circles under her eyes, put there probably by fatigue and tears and days of terror. She was heavily bruised wherever Fargo could see her skin.

Until now Fargo had felt disgust for the men, anger, even contempt for the kind of men they were.

Now, confronted with their victim, he felt a deep, icy hatred that churned inside him. Men like that had no business walking on the face of this earth.

The Trailsman swore that he would see that they walked the earth and breathed its air for not one moment longer than he could help.

He stood and went to the mare, took down one of the canteens Jim Nelson had given him, and pulled off his bandana.

He knelt beside the woman again and with the moistened cloth began tenderly to bathe her face and wash her. He was going to have to remove her dress if he expected to find and to pull all the thorns that had been stabbed deep into her flesh. He hoped that wouldn't embarrass her.

But at least now, and with luck forever more, she would not be handled by any cowardly son of a bitch who wanted to use and to harm her. Never again. Certainly not by those three murdering rapists.

Those three were already as good as dead, the way Fargo figured it.

The Trailsman had already judged them and found them guilty.

The sentence was death by execution.

All the rest of it was just a matter of detail.

8

The woman remained unconscious throughout the afternoon. Fargo bathed her and pulled all the pricklypear stickers he could locate, then painted the most obvious of her wounds with a sweet-smelling balm that he found in one of the packs Calder and his men had abandoned—he hoped it was a medication; it looked like something that should help—and completely redressed her without her ever knowing any of it.

She had no injuries that looked like they should have left her unconscious so long, basically just the slash across the face and some older bruises. He was beginning to think she must have hit her head when she fell off the horse, although he could find no goose-egg bumps under her hair that would fit with that notion. It was worrisome.

After a while he left her long enough to hobble the pack horses and the unattended saddle horses, the poor one she had been riding and the much better pair that had belonged to the men Fargo had killed, Razz Berry and his quiet partner. He also checked the two dead men for their part of the bank loot, but their pockets were empty except for ammunition. Fargo appropriated their revolvers—it was beginning to look like spares could come in mighty handy in this country—but left them unburied. The hell with that. They didn't deserve it.

Even after all that, the woman was still out cold. Fargo had begun to suspect that she might be passed out not from injury but as a means of escape from the horrors she had been put through of late. He had heard of such things happening before. For all he knew, she might wake up crazy as a june bug.

Late in the afternoon, fretting still because Calder and what was left of his gang were pulling more and more of a lead on him, Fargo accepted the idea that he wouldn't be doing any more traveling this day. He couldn't ride off and leave the woman passed out on the prairie, dammit.

While he still had time enough before the darkness that would give him away to any Comanche, he built a tiny, almost smokeless fire from roots and dried twigs and some pellets of old deer droppings, then put a can of water over the flames to heat. He shaved *carne seca* into the water and cooked it into a thin broth that he could keep ready for her if she ever woke. She needed strength, he figured, and the broth would be good for her even cold.

The contents of the packs must have come from the wagons and from the Walters place, because Fargo had watched the gang ride out of San Antonio unencumbered by pack horses that day. Calder had been damned lucky in what he'd stolen since then. There was plenty of the *carne seca* and some cornmeal, even a little wheat flour, cooking utensils, extra blankets. He used the blankets to make a bed for the girl and added some cornmeal to the hot broth to thicken and enrich it.

Now all he needed was for her to wake up so he could get on with the business of . . . What the hell was he going to do with her? He couldn't leave her out here, even if she jumped up grinning and healthy. And it was a hell of a distance to the nearest settlement that he knew of, days of riding in any direction.

Fargo kicked the fire apart before it was full dark and sat beside the dying coals to watch and wait, helpless to act while every minute Calder and his men drew farther and farther away from him.

Judging from the wheel of the stars overhead—higher in the sky here than he was accustomed to but nonetheless familiar—it was ten o'clock or later before the woman stirred in her deep, near-death sleep.

Fargo had been dozing, but he was alert and sitting upright instantly, that bit of movement enough to alert him.

His immediate inclination was to rush to her, but he stopped himself. The way she'd been treated by strangers lately, she was more likely to take that as another attack than the offer of help he truly intended. Instead, he forced himself to sit where he was on his blanket, an arm's length from her, and speak gently. "Are you feeling better now?"

She didn't respond, but in the dim light of the stars and moon he could see that her eyes were wide open and bright. She stared at him unblinking. It was unnatural.

But then nothing that had happened to her had been natural of late, Fargo reminded himself.

He sat cross-legged, facing her but not touching her, and began to talk like they were having a perfectly normal conversation.

"My name is Skye," he told her. "Those other, uh, fellows, the ones that hurt you and your family"—there was no point in trying to avoid mention of that; she damn sure wouldn't be forgetting it, so there was no sense in him mousing around about it either—"they won't be coming back. They won't hurt you again. Not ever." Still she didn't speak or so much as blink. "Do you understand what I'm telling you? You're safe now. You won't be hurt anymore. All that's over with. Nobody's going to hurt you now. Not ever again, if I have anything to say about it."

There was no response. She had rolled her head so that she could see in his direction, and her eyes were wide open and staring. But she didn't react in any way to what he was telling her.

The Trailsman's experience with frightened women was not exactly great. Maybe, he decided, she needed to be petted and gentled, like a nervous horse. Or, more to the point, the way he always soothed and reassured any woman. Maybe he should stroke the back of her head, smooth down her hair, even hold her and rock her and pat her shoulders. He shifted to her side.

Oh, hell. Oh, Lordy! Skye Fargo was chilled with horror at what the poor damn woman did when he approached her like that, thinking only to comfort and help her.

She rolled her head to the other side so that those wide, staring eyes were pointed away from him. And she parted her legs in acceptance of the inevitability of rape.

She was an unhappy thing. Her eyes were wide as a doe's, soft. All the rest of her was tiny. She was so little and so skinny he thought he could put the fingers of one hand all the way around that thin little neck. He'd seen her when he bathed her, of course. He knew that there wasn't much more to her anyplace else.

He wanted to reach out to her, touch her and comfort her, and . . . somehow make it all go away.

But he couldn't. There just wasn't a damn thing that he could do to help that she might not interpret as being something entirely else. There wasn't anything he could do that mightn't make her think of those foul animals who'd turned her into this . . . this scared thing she seemed to have become.

Lord Almighty, Fargo thought.

He returned to his own blanket and sat cross-legged there, talking to her, not saying anything important or anything particular, just talking nonsensical stuff. Reassuring her, telling funny stories he could remember from his own travels or just jokes—the few clean ones that he could recall—that he'd heard from time to time.

Soft, gentle-toned talking gave her a voice to hear that wasn't threatening her with harm.

He talked to her like that for some hours through the night.

But she never once moved and never once rolled her head back to be looking in his direction.

Somewhere around two in the morning he gave it up and let his voice trail away into the stillness of the night. He lay down and closed his eyes, but even so, it was a while before he could get back to sleep.

"I think you'll like this," Fargo said cheerfully. He smiled. "It tastes better than it looks. Honestly."

He held out a handful of the honey-fruit-nut mixture Jane had devised and waited patiently until the silent, wide-eyed woman looked over the stuff with suspicion and finally extended her cupped hands to accept the breakfast. Fargo considered that simple thing a major breakthrough. The woman had actually accepted something he offered her. That was a first.

He grinned at her and put the rest of the stuff away in his saddlebags. He hadn't much of it left now, and he thought it would be better for the woman than the *carne seca*, which he took out for his own breakfast. He didn't want to take the time or risk the smoke to cook anything, so these dried foods would have to do.

"Do you feel up to riding this morning? We need to find someplace where you'll be safe," he said, ignoring the fact that she made no response to his words.

He continued to talk to her while he went about the routine chores of saddling the brown for himself and the better of the two dead men's horses for the woman, then made up the packs and lashed them onto the makeshift pack frames Calder had been using. It was a rough but workable arrangement. He would take along the two saddle horses and the pack horses. The loose animals could follow along or not. Although that probably wasn't fair to the woman. You could make a case for them being her property. Selling them someplace might give her a few dollars toward her keep. Though how she was going to be kept, and by whom, was going to be an interesting problem, particularly if she didn't start talking again. Maybe she would when he got her to another woman.

"You probably know how to do this," he chattered while he worked. "See? We put this line over here and bring it back across to here . . . and then we knot it here, and here . . . and go back to the other side and knot it again here and over here. And that should hold just fine. See?"

She stared at him in silence. Her eyes were large and unblinking, her face slack and expressionless. Fargo pretended that they were getting along just fine.

"Do you need some help into the saddle? I can lift you if you like."

She was hearing him just fine. Just not responding worth a damn. She went and crawled into the saddle by herself, having to shinny up the stirrup leathers and pull herself onto the horse but doing it with silent determination. Fargo let her be. She likely would have jumped out of her skin if he'd laid a hand on her to help.

She sat on the leather seat of the saddle like a lump of cheese, making no move to take up her reins. For all he knew, maybe she'd never ridden a horse by herself before.

Fargo rigged a lead rope on her horse and fixed the leads of the pack horses to the flank cinch D-ring on her saddle so that he could ride the brown and lead the whole outfit at once.

It was a helluva way to travel when a man was after a gang of robbing, murdering fiends. But he couldn't see that he had much choice about it.

"What I've been thinking," he said pleasantly, continuing the one-sided conversation that had been going on ever since the woman wakened this morning, "is that we ought to head for El Paso del Norte. It isn't all that much out of the way, like going back to the Texas settlements would be. And maybe we'll luck into a homestead or something when we get closer. It's either that or going on across to Fort Union. Or turning back all the way to Fredericksburg. That's about the closest town to the east that I know about, you see, and I've never actually been there. So I could miss it if we went east again."

He kneed the brown into a slow walk, with the string of led horses coming awkwardly behind. "Wouldn't want to do that, as I've business to the west. So I thought we'd head for El Paso del Norte. Fort Union might be just a bit closer, but we'd have to cross the Llano to get there, and that mightn't be safe. So I really think we want to try for El Paso del Norte. Unless, of course, you got kinfolk somewhere that I could take you to. But I wouldn't know about that. Be willing, if you do, though." He had accepted the fact that he should ask her no direct questions. But if she wanted to speak, that would be just fine. Be a damn sight better if she would, but there was no sense in pushing her for it. That would just make it all worse.

They rode slowly west, angling off to the south now. It graveled Fargo to have to leave the tracks laid down by Calder and his men. But there was no help for that either. The woman was his responsibility now until he could get her to a place of safekeeping. He damn sure couldn't take her with him into the muzzles of Calder's guns. She'd been through enough without that.

"What we'll do," he said as they neared the buttes he thought the gang had been moving toward yesterday, "is swing to the north just a little here so we can come down along the east face of these buttes. We're getting a little low on water. Nothing to be worried about, of course. Still got a little left in that one canteen. But that isn't enough for us and the horses, not even for today. So we'd best see if we can find a tank and everybody drink up. If we find enough water and you want a bath, I can stand off a ways and let you clean up on your own. Might make you feel some better if you can do that."

He turned in his saddle to look at her and found her wide, bright eyes fixed on him. But her expression didn't change from its blank, empty stare, and she continued to say nothing at all. He had no damned idea if she wanted a bath or not. And there was no point in asking outright. If she took one, he would figure she'd wanted one. If she didn't, she didn't.

He rode on, wishing to hell Jane had told him where Calder was headed. That sure would have made things better now that he couldn't follow behind them.

"So," Fargo said later in the same pleasant, cheerfully chatty voice he'd been using right along, "here is where we have to decide for sure. Either we head up that way"—he pointed to the northwest—"for Fort Union. Or we cut south of some mountains up ahead. Can't see them yet, but they're there. And then we angle off to El Paso, which is someplace down that way." He pointed again, this time to the south.

He was pretty sure of where the mountains were. Not exactly, perhaps, but in general. There were supposed to be some low, rugged, very dry small mountains somewhere ahead of them. The Guadalupes, some called them. Others said they were the Sacramentos. Whatever the name, Fargo wanted to avoid them.

"If you have a preference," he said, "now is the time to show it. Otherwise, we head down toward El Paso." He turned in the saddle and smiled back toward the woman. "Be good to have some hot coffee and cooked food when we get there, whichever place. Maybe some candy too. Or dried-apple pie. I sure have been hankering dried-apple pie lately, and I'll bet you'd like some of that too."

She stared vacantly forward, looking neither right nor left, seeming not to care whether they went to Union or El Paso.

She had been like that for the better part of two days now, silent and expressionless. Sitting her saddle with all the cheery animation of a bucket of rancid suet, with both hands clasped on the horn and her scrawny legs poking out to the sides, she never even made the effort to put her feet into the stirrups, just sat there perched on the slick leather seat and let Fargo lead her wherever he chose.

Yet when he offered food, she took it. When he gave her an instruction, which he did as seldom as possible, she followed it. She moved with slow, wooden deliberation. But she did follow his instructions and comply with his requests, so she heard. She wasn't crazy, exactly. She just seemed to have withdrawn to someplace where he couldn't follow and from which she emerged only rarely, and never fully.

"Okay, Junebug," he said. During the past two days he had taken to calling her that for no better reason than that he wanted to be able to call her something. He still had no idea of what her name was. He had yet to hear her voice. Unless you counted the sounds she made late in the night when he would wake to hear her sobbing in near silence from the privacy of the blankets that she invariably drew completely over her head regardless of the heat.

"What we'll do," he went on as naturally as if they were having a normal, two-sided conversation, "is head off that way. Down toward El Paso del Norte." He smiled at her again. "They tell me that means Pass of the North. Or to the north, I'm not sure which. But maybe you knew that already."

Junebug said nothing. Her sight remained fixed somewhere in front of them.

"El Paso it is, then," Fargo said cheerfully. He nudged the brown mare into motion again. Immediately behind him Junebug's horse moved to follow and the two pack horses behind it. And past them, the other loose stock followed as well. The whole herd had remained together from the instincts of protection in numbers, although any of them had been free to break off on their own if they liked. That was a mixed blessing. Fargo was pleased that the small herd would be intact when they got where they were going. He figured to sell the animals on Junebug's behalf and put the money toward her keep with some likely family. On the other hand, having so many animals moving together raised a dust, even at the slow speed he was making.

It was a trade-off but one he could do little about short of shooting some of the horses to drive the others away. And he wasn't willing to do that. It could harm the woman. Not just by costing her that money for her keep, but maybe the sight of blood and the sounds of the shooting would disturb her. He still wasn't sure what would bother her and what she would just ignore. Once, without thinking, he had touched her on the shoulder to get her attention when he wanted to give her a bit of choice, salt-crusted jerky. She reacted to the touch like he'd taken a damn whip to her. That was a mistake he hadn't made a second time, but there was no telling what else might frighten her. He was trying to take as few chances as possible with her.

They moved slowly on through the harsh glare of the afternoon sun. Fargo was thinking, trying to decide. There was a coach road somewhere to the south. The southern crossing from Texas all the way to California. If he headed south for a spell he was bound to cut that road. And along it there would be relay stations where the stages changed teams. Those stations would mean people, maybe even a place where he could leave

Junebug and get back to the business of finding the sons of bitches that had made her like this.

But a traveled road, too, would mean the possibility of being jumped by raiding parties of Comanches or Apaches or whatever. Any wild tribes, or white robbers, or Mexican bandits would do their hunting along that road. He didn't want to expose Junebug to trouble if he could avoid it.

He sighed quietly to himself—maybe this silent bullshit was catching—and moved steadily forward, the herd of loose horses trailing docilely behind.

They traveled forward in silence, the dry earth passing beneath them for hours until the Trailsman drew rein.

"Look over there," Fargo said, pointing. "There's a wash or gully. Arroyo they might call it here. Couldn't see it before, but if you pay attention, Junebug, you can just make out the difference. Like with the shadow of that tall, whippy mesquite that's setting off by itself. See right over there? That one. If you look close, you can see the way the shadow lies across the ground and then disappears. But it doesn't look like the ground should be falling away just there. Yet it does. So we figure there's an arroyo over there that we couldn't see till now because of the lay of the land. And being cautious folk, Junebug, you and me will ride wide around that, because in this kind of country you just never want to quit being careful. If you got any choice about it at all, you just kind of avoid places where someone could be laying an ambush."

Junebug didn't answer. But then he hadn't expected a response.

Fargo reined the brown to the right, and the rest of the horses followed. He stifled a yawn—he hadn't been sleeping all that good of late—and cast a wary look back in the direction of the hidden arroyo.

"Oh, shit," he blurted.

A clump of sage he had been looking at suddenly

changed shape, became thicker, fuller, rose up off the baked caliche soil, and yipped a sharp cry of warning.

A second more and the rim of the hidden wash was solid Indians. The red men were shrieking and brandishing bows and lances and a few rifles and charging like hell toward Fargo and the woman. The lances were long and looked awkward, almost silly, because all the Indians were on foot. They had remained hidden until Fargo turned his line of travel. Now they were out in the open and charging as hard as they could run toward the two whites.

"Hang on, Junebug," Fargo shouted. He dug his spurs into the brown's flank and jumped her forward.

They were in no danger. There might have been if they had come close enough to that shallow wash. But they hadn't. Fargo had seen it and turned off in plenty of time. With the Indians on foot, Fargo and the woman could outrun them without hardly raising a sweat.

He was assessing that automatically, not even pulling a revolver, thinking about how far they would have to ride this evening to make sure they were safe from pursuit by the dismounted Indians.

Then the whole damn thing went sour.

The gelding Junebug was mounted on was taken by surprise when Fargo jumped the brown mare forward. It felt the sudden jerk of the lead rope and balked.

The brown mare felt the pull of the lead rope dragging her back against the conflicting command of Fargo's spurs. She snorted and threw her head and began to buck.

"Not now, dammit," Fargo snapped. He whipped his rein ends back and forth across her shoulders, trying to keep an eye on the hard-running Indians while he did so. They weren't as far away as they had been. There wasn't time to be assing around here with a snorty horse. He punched her with the spurs again, damn sure meaning it this time.

Again the mare tried to bolt forward in response to

the command. But again the forward motion, coming immediately after her more or less stationary bucking, took Junebug's gelding by surprise.

This time the damn gelding took to bucking.

And the woman wasn't a rider. She was just a passenger who happened to be sitting on the fool horse's saddle. She didn't so much as have her feet in the stirrups.

Junebug came unglued at the gelding's first lurch, flying loose from the saddle and coming down hard on her back. Even from where he sat on the brown mare, Fargo could hear the air whoosh out of her lungs when she hit the ground.

Indians were almighty close now, close enough that they were beginning to shoot.

Fuck this, Fargo told himself. He snatched the lead rope loose from the mare and tossed it aside. Led animals would only slow them down, and right now they couldn't afford a whole hell of a lot more of that.

He wheeled the brown to Junebug and leaned low off his saddle with his hand extended. He could grab up the woman, throw her over the brown with him, and get the hell out of there before one of those war-whooping redskins got lucky.

She lay where she was, gasping for breath, not reaching up to take his hand. He didn't know if she didn't see him, or if she was refusing to touch him. Either way it could get her killed.

"Grab . . . Forget it."

He jumped down off the mare, keeping a firm hold on his reins, and snatched at her arm.

She jerked away from him, turning bellydown on the hard ground and trying to crawl off away from him. She was making small mewling, whining sounds of fear somewhere deep in her throat.

Jesus!

An arrow thunked into the earth a couple yards to their right and then another, closer. Those Indians weren't much with firearms, not yet anyway, but they were hell with a bow.

"We haven't got time for this." Fargo had to run the damn woman down, dragging the nervous and once again snorty mare behind him, waddling forward astraddle of the squirming woman, trying to get a hold on her and keep the mare under control at the same time.

This wasn't the time to be playing nicey-nice. Every time he'd try to grab one of her wrists or arms or whatever, she would tuck the damn thing underneath her and roll aside, bumping into Fargo's legs and almost knocking him down. Left, left, right, left. Every time she got away from him. And the arrows were coming thick and fast now. It was only dumb luck that neither of them had been hit so far.

He grabbed for the middle, sinking his fist into the woman's hair—he could apologize for hurting her damn feelings some other time—and hauled her onto her feet. She was screaming too now, her voice joining with that of the closing Indians. She was hissing and kicking and twisting like a cat that doesn't want to be held.

Fargo didn't have time to worry about that now. He hauled her upright, took a wrap around her skinny body with one arm—who the hell would have thought such a little bit of a thing would've been such a scrapper? —and tried to get a foot into the mare's stirrup.

It was definitely time to find a new piece of country.

An arrow hit the seat of his saddle practically under Fargo's nose as he was still trying to get a boot into the stirrup. The wickedly pointed tip sliced through the leather, missed the flats of his hardwood tree somehow, and pierced the mare's back.

He could see now that she'd been hit several times already on the other side. The mare had been shielding them from some of the arrows, and he hadn't realized it.

Fargo turned loose of her reins, still fighting to try to

keep the spitting, clawing Junebug under his arm, and ran for the gelding that the woman had abandoned.

"Oh, shit!"

The gelding shied away, snorted once with its ears pinned flat, and took off at a high run for calmer parts, dragging the two pack horses with it.

Fargo tried to turn back for the mare. A dying horse was better than a dead one. Just a mile or two would . . .

The mare coughed and went to her knees, blood trickling out of her flaring nostrils.

The Indians were damn close now. Just a few yards away.

Fargo dropped the kicking woman, turned loose of her, and let her fall. He grabbed for his revolvers. If he was going to go down, dammit, he wasn't going to do it easy.

A Colt in each hand, the Trailsman squared off to face the charge.

A high-flung lance came arcing down out of the sun. He barely had half a moment to register the fact that it was there. Then the crude weapon struck him just above the hairline, and the world turned muzzily black and distant.

Fargo fell facedown in the dirt with his revolvers unfired and a whimpering woman now clutching tight to his legs.

9

He hurt. Lordy, but he hurt.

The top of his head felt like it had been split apart. He turned his head a little, not trusting himself to open his eyes just yet, and felt the itch and pull of dried blood crusted across the whole right side of his face and in his ear and down his neck inside his shirt.

For a moment he couldn't remember. Then it came back to him. Junebug, the Indians, that lance coming down out of the sky, the fight . . .

Fight? Hell, there hadn't been a fight.

A bunch of damn Indians running on foot, not a horse in sight, and they'd taken him without any kind of a fight at all. It was disgusting. If it hadn't been for Junebug . . .

Fargo's eyes snapped wide open. The woman! Where the hell was she?

He tried to rise, ignoring the sharp pains that shot through his skull at the motion. Only then did he focus on the dull pain in his hands and wrists and realize where it came from.

Sometime while he was out, the Indians had bound his hands behind him, and his feet too.

He was trussed like a shoat waiting for slaughter.

Slaughter. That was an interesting thought. Why the hell hadn't they killed him? And where was the woman?

Fargo blinked. His vision was blurred, probably as a result of the knock he had taken on the head. He blinked again, harder, and shook his head. It felt like somebody had emptied out his brains and substituted a couple hundredweight of cannon balls that were rolling around inside there, slamming off the sides of his skull every time he moved. Dammit. But at least after a bit he was able to get his eyes to focus again.

He was lying near the Indian encampment. They looked to be more Comanche, although he wasn't positive about that. The last time he had seen Comanche, they had been painted for war. None of these was painted, and they weren't stripped to their breech-clouts and amulets for combat either. The men wore shirts and leggings, and there were women among them too. Fargo tried to remember the visual differences between Comanche and Apache, but at the moment he couldn't. He kept looking around trying to spot Junebug.

He was responsible for her, dammit. So where was she?

He couldn't see her.

It was evening. Still early evening, though, he thought. There was still sun heat in the ground. And something in the smell of the air, undefinable in his groggy, foggy state, that hinted the night wasn't far advanced.

The Comanche had built a large fire and a number of smaller cooking fires. They seemed to be celebrating something. Well, that was reasonable enough. They'd damn sure come out on top of their ambush this afternoon. They were entitled to some celebrating.

Most of the men were busy with the horse herd, which was close to the camp. They were handling the animals, feeding them. Now and then one of the warriors would rig a rein on a horse—not a bit like a white man would use but a single cord or rope knotted on the horse's jaw—and jump onto it to ride briefly away from the vicinity of the cooking pots. The Comanche had the common-sense courtesy of not raising dust around food. They put each animal through its paces, wheeling and spinning the creature, then riding back to the rest where maybe another man would jump onto the horse and try it out.

There was something odd about that, but it took Fargo a befuddled moment or two—he must have been cracked harder than he'd realized—to work out what it was.

Then he looked again and saw that the only horses in sight were ones that had been with him and Junebug. All were animals Calder and his gang had ridden away from San Antonio or stolen since then. There wasn't a single Indian pony anywhere around.

That explained that, Fargo thought. The Comanche had all been afoot when they came out of that shallow wash. Somewhere along their way this raid of theirs had gone just about as sour as Fargo's nonfight today. They had lost their horse herd.

No doubt they had been tickled pink to see a white man and girl and bunch of loose horses come walking right to them.

And they were all the happier to get their hands on those horses when by rights there wasn't any way in the world it should have happened.

Dammit. If only Junebug . . .

Fargo shook his head again, this time angry with himself. He kept getting distracted, drifting off one train of thought and jumping willy-nilly into another.

That wasn't doing anyone any good.

He closed his eyes for a moment and lay silently, marshaling his strength and trying to regain full control of his faculties.

Fargo felt no false illusions about his situation here. Or the woman's, wherever the hell she was.

The Comanche hadn't kept him alive as a gesture of mercy or sweet reason. Their first priority had been getting the horses the band needed for survival in this hostile land. Their second would have been their women. And now a meal.

Likely they intended to get around to chopping him up at their leisure, once the really important things were tended to.

Was it the Comanches who liked to stake men out over anthills with their faces turned toward the sun and their eyelids cut off? Or was that the Apaches? He couldn't remember at the moment, which was probably just as well. He was drifting again, his thoughts veering off on their own.

Fargo lay still for a moment, then tensed, his muscles cording and straining. The bite of the rawhide was cruel on his flesh. That much was all right. What he minded was that the cord didn't give, not by a fraction of an inch. Whoever had bound him had done an almighty good job of it.

He tried again, but it was no good.

He thought about rolling away from the camp, rolling over and over until he gained a little distance from the circles of firelight, then squirming away somehow, wriggling off on his belly. Maybe eventually he could find a rock and abrade the rawhide until it parted. Then maybe he could come back and try to help the woman. If both of them remained here, it would do neither of them any good. He had to be able to get away in order for her to have a chance.

Wherever the hell she was.

He raised his head and looked for her again.

She didn't seem to be anywhere near the fires.

For sure she wasn't with the men over by the horses.

Fargo felt a block of ice develop deep in his gut. He hadn't seen it before. But over there . . . past the horses . . . past that group of warriors . . . over beyond them, there was another, small group of Comanche.

Men, younger than the ones around the horses. Young bucks. One of them was just getting to his feet. The son of a bitch was tucking his pecker back into his breechclout. And saying something to his pals. The rest of them laughed at whatever the young one had just said. Then one of them dropped his breechclout, exposing a stand-tall erection, and dropped down onto something . . . someone.

Fargo had too good an idea of who that would have to be.

The poor woman hadn't suffered enough from Calder and his men.

Fargo struggled against the rawhide bindings. He pulled and twisted until blood ran from his wrists, but there was no escape. Not for him. Not for poor Junebug.

He squeezed his eyes tight shut in fury and frustration and struggled all the harder.

The rawhide held, trapping him, immobilizing him.

From just beyond the horse herd he heard a sudden, anguished cry.

It was the first real sound he had ever heard from the girl.

And the last.

A girl approached him. She was pretty, with long black hair and large dark eyes. She wore a doeskin dress decorated with dyed porcupine quills in a pattern of red and black and ivory. She was carrying a chunk of greasy, half-cooked meat. Fargo knew what the meat was. He had seen one of the men bring in a bunch of huge lizards a while ago. Chuckwallas, he thought they were called. They were ugly, but the meat looked good. It was pale, almost like chicken. Fargo looked at it and his mouth began to water. He was damned hungry, and a fried scorpion would have been welcome. Well, almost.

The Comanche girl smiled down at him, and Fargo

brightened. If she was willing to feed him, maybe she could be talked into freeing him too. Stranger things than that had happened.

He greeted her.

She said something back in a strange tongue and squatted in front of him. The hem of her light, leather dress rode high on her thighs when she did so. She had nice legs. It was too dark to be sure, but he thought she was not wearing anything under the doeskin garment.

Interesting possibilities.

He looked hungrily at both the girl and the meat she had in her hands. If he could get her to help him . . .

His eyes swept away from the Comanche girl and beyond her to where the young warriors had finished their sport with Junebug some little while back. He never had actually seen her over there. Obviously she was lying on the ground too, and he was too low to be able to see that far. He assumed they'd tied her up and left her there until they wanted her again.

The Comanche girl said something else, and his attention was pulled back to her.

She smiled and Fargo smiled up at her. He could feel a swelling at his crotch.

The Indian girl saw. She laughed and spoke.

Amused, she said something more, then raised the meat—damn, but it looked and smelled fine even if it was nothing but a lizard—to her own mouth. She took a bite and swallowed, then another, turning the thin bone in her fingers and gnawing the last scraps of meat from it.

She tossed the bone into the brush and wiped grease-slick fingers along her thighs. The grease she left behind there was caught in the light from the fires, shining bright and returning Fargo's attention to what she seemed to be showing him. His erection got harder.

The girl laughed again and shifted forward, closer to him. She bent down and unbuttoned his shirt, exposing his chest. Then she spread the cloth wide and said something. He was sure wishing she spoke English or that he could figure out the grunting and croaking of her dialect. But this would have to do.

Smiling, the Indian girl ran a finger across his chest, down over his ribs, and back up on his belly. She said something more and teased his nipples.

Then, still smiling, she reached into a pouch hung from a cord tied at her waist and brought out a small, very sharp knife.

Fargo grinned back at her. This was better than he could have hoped. He rolled onto his side to offer her his hands, tied behind his back.

The girl pressed the flat of her free hand against his chest and rolled him onto his back again.

She wasn't smiling now.

With a swift, unexpected motion she swept the razor edge of the knifeblade across his chest, slicing shallowly into his flesh.

The wound didn't hurt so much as it surprised him. "What the hell . . .?"

Lips compressed now and face impassive, the Comanche girl cut him again. Blood swelled out of both cuts to spread out onto his chest and run down over his belly. She returned the little knife to her pouch and dipped her fingertips into the warmth of the fresh blood.

She slapped him then, Hard, splattering his own blood across his face.

With a harsh parting word that it was probably just as well he couldn't understand, the girl stood and stalked away toward the other Comanches.

Fargo got the impression, though, that she would be back.

He began to sweat, the sweat mixing with the blood on his chest and chilling him in the night air, stinging him where it oozed into the fresh cuts. He squeezed his eyes shut.

The Trailsman no longer had an erection.

Things could have been worse, he supposed. He could already be dead.

But he expected to take that final step any old time now. The question was when, not whether.

He tried straining against the bonds again, thinking that perhaps the blood from his wrists would be enough moisture to soften the rawhide and allow him to stretch it. Just a little stretching would do, just enough to let him get his hands free.

Hell's bells, if he could only get his hands free, just his hands. He would settle for that. He would almost be willing to make a bargain to that effect. Let him get his hands loose and he wouldn't ask for any more. He wouldn't demand to have his feet freed also.

All right, he told himself. He wouldn't exactly agree to not try to free his feet. That would be a lie, not a bargain. But if he couldn't, well, he wouldn't complain about it. Just so he could get his hands loose and fight back, dammit.

That was what was getting to him the worst. So far he hadn't done anything to help himself. Or to help that poor Junebug.

She was over there in the brush somewhere. He couldn't see her. He was glad he couldn't. He wouldn't have been able to look the poor kid in the eyes. Damn. He'd been responsible for her, and he'd let her down, let her get taken and used like that.

He hadn't seen her since the Comanche took the two of them. Hadn't heard her except that once.

Now even the young bucks were ignoring her. The women and the older men had ignored her right along, but now there was no interest in her at all that he could see.

She must be scared to death, lying over there all alone in the dark with her hands and feet tied. She was also probably resenting the Trailsman and his failure to keep her safe.

Fargo pulled at the bindings around his wrists again. There was no meager hint of release whatsoever.

Damn!

He was beginning to think that the Comanche weren't as dumb as he hoped. Maybe they hadn't tied him with rawhide, after all. Hell, he couldn't actually see the stuff. It just felt like it. But surely by now rawhide would have been releasing as it got wet. It did that quite predictably, stretching when it was wet and contracting as it dried. But not this stuff. For damn sure he'd gotten it wet enough from his bleeding.

A little blood would be a small-enough price to pay if it would help him get loose. But this didn't seem to be working.

He tried again, with no more success than before.

A little more of this shit, Fargo thought, and a fellow could tend toward discouragement.

One of the young Comanches wandered over in his direction, satisfying himself that the white man was still there, and booted Fargo in the ribs.

Fargo grunted but managed to keep from crying out. It hurt, but there were things that hurt worse, like thinking about Junebug. He lay looking up at the Comanche buck. He willed the son of a bitch to fall over dead. If cold looks could have done the job, the boy would have died on the spot.

The kid—he couldn't have been a whole hell of a lot older than fourteen tops—gave Fargo a smug, nasty look and kicked him again. He said something in the same tongue the girl had used, then walked cockily back toward the fire and his supper.

Fargo struggled at his bonds again, but still the cord, rope, leather, whatever, held firm.

If only he could get his hands free . . . just his hands. At this point he would have been willing to strike that bargain and swear to leave his feet tied if only he could have his hands to fight back with.

He grunted. Damn them. But if he had nothing else, dammit, when they came he'd bite. Infect 'em, if nothing else, and hope for gangrene to set in after he was dead and gone.

He lay there for a while wondering if there might be some way he could work it so he could get a chomp at more than just one of them when they came.

"Psssst!"

Fargo grunted and stirred.

"Pssst!"

He tried to sit up but couldn't. His head was still hurting, his chest stung like hell, his ribs ached where that little asshole had kicked him, and he was dizzy, probably from loss of blood. He'd had better days and either dozed off or passed out for a while there.

"Psssst!"

There was that sound again. He shook his head to try to clear it.

"Pssst, dammit."

Now that was something else again. He wiggled around so that he could see in that direction, sure now that he wasn't imagining things.

"Junebug?" he whispered.

"Who the hell is Junebug?" The whisper was in a voice that was vaguely familiar, although he couldn't place it. It was a woman's voice. It almost had to be Junebug. But then he'd never heard her speak before, so how could her voice be familiar to him? He was trying to puzzle that out, still too woozy to manage much in the line of clear thinking, when she crawled closer and he got a look at her.

"Jane?"

"Yes. Shut up and turn around."

"But—"

"We don't have time for a visit, Skye. Now roll over so I can get at those cords."

Jane was supposed to be a couple hundred miles

east. Not here. He almost argued with her that she couldn't be here, then thought better of it and rolled over as instructed.

He felt a sharp tug at the ropes that were holding his hands, then they separated. He was free. Lord Almighty, his hands were free. Jane moved down to his feet and slashed again. Hot damn, he was completely loose now.

His hands and feet felt like a bed of ants had been asleep inside them and had all come awake at once. It was almost worse than the aching in his head and in his ribs.

He tried to get up, but Jane restrained him. "Stay down, you idiot. They'll see you. Keep low and follow me, Skye. Stay right behind me."

He wanted to argue with her. There were things he needed to do at the Comanche camp.

For just a moment he couldn't remember what those things were. He had to concentrate hard on it. Then it came to him, and he stopped Jane. She had already begun to crawl out into the night.

"The woman," he whispered into her ear. "I've got to go back and get her. The one I named Junebug. She's a little gone in the head, and—"

"Shush," Jane told him. "You're getting too loud."

"But—"

She put a hand on his arm. "You can't do anything for her, Skye."

"But—"

"Skye. Please." Her expression was pained and sympathetic. "She's dead, Skye. I . . . I crawled over there to check on her. After they'd gone. Believe me, Skye, you don't want to see her. Now shut up and follow me. We don't have all that much time before they get down to the meat of the celebration, Skye. And that happens to be you."

Fargo shut up and let Jane lead him away from the camp, both of them crawling silently on their bellies.

It was a hell of an ignominious way to be leaving.

On the other hand, he was leaving . . . alive.

He wasn't in great shape and he still didn't know what in hell Jane was doing out here, but he wasn't complaining, either.

The two of them slipped quietly off into the protection of the darkness.

10

Fargo and Jane were huddled together, the two of them occupying a space barely large enough for one, under the bank of the wash where the Comanche had hidden earlier in the day. Jane had dragged up some brush and driftwood to cover them with. The sun wasn't yet up but already they could hear the yelps and complaints of the warriors who were looking for their escaped prisoner. Fargo was still in lousy shape.

"I still think it would have been easier to steal a damn horse. Lord knows, you're a good-enough thief for the job." He shifted position a little, seeking comfort. What he got was an acute awareness of her body pressed against his.

What he said, though, was certainly true enough. In addition to coming into the Comanche camp to cut Fargo free, Jane had also stolen a canteen, a pouch of dried corn, a magnifying glass, and a pair of moccasins that looked like they would fit Fargo.

Instead of answering his implied question, she explored the gash on his head with gentle fingertips. "You're still almost out of it, aren't you, Skye?"

"I don't see what that has to do with—"

"Keep your voice down. We don't want them to find us now," she said. "I think you have a fever. Here." She pulled the cork from the neck of the blanket-sided canteen and gave him a swallow of the tepid water. It tasted better than any liquor he had ever had.

"But—"

"Hush. I already told you, Skye. I couldn't steal all the horses. They were too closely guarded. And horses leave tracks. Moccasins don't. Not on ground this hard. If we can get away on foot, we'll be safe. If we tried to run without having taken their every last horse, they could come after us, find us again. I want to get away from them, Skye. They frighten me. Believe me, I should know them. I lived with their kind long enough. I even remember some of this band. We wintered with them twice. Up in the Palo Duro, that was." She shuddered and Fargo held her closer.

"Okay, but what the hell are you doing here?"

"I told you that back at Norman's place, Skye. I'm going after those men. I already told you that."

Fargo shook his head. He'd thought Jane safe back at the settlements all this time. Instead, she had been walking—walking, for crying out loud—the whole time, chasing the damned Calder outfit on foot.

And aside from not having a horse, the fool girl hadn't anything else in the way of equipment either. She had set off in the flimsy dress she'd been wearing when he saw her before but with the skirt hacked short so it wouldn't interfere with movement, quickly and crudely homemade moccasins, and with a small pouch and a butcher knife as her only gear. With no more than that she intended to take on half a dozen armed men.

She was crazy as hell, Fargo figured.

Not that he was complaining. She had also pulled him out of a fix back there at the Indian camp.

But she had gotten herself into one too. The results

weren't quite in on that one and wouldn't be until the Comanches either found them or gave up and went away.

If Fargo were just feeling up to some hard travel . . . But he wasn't. Not yet. He had been thumped on just too thoroughly in too many ways. That was one thing he had to concede that Jane was right about: He was in no shape to travel quite yet. And dawn was awfully near now. With nothing but the girl's knife to defend them, getting caught out in the open by a bunch of Comanches probably wouldn't be a good plan.

Plan? Shit. His head was hurting so bad he could hardly think, much less make sensible plans. At least he was beginning to realize that himself now. That was an improvement, wasn't it?

He sighed and shifted again, seeking a more comfortable position inside the impossibly small hidey-hole she had found.

Her breasts pressed against him through the thin cloth that separated their bodies, and her breath was warm on his neck where she nuzzled close to him.

Hurting though he was, Fargo's reaction was strong and decidedly male.

Jane must have felt the swell of his interest. She grinned at him with a wicked little twist to her mouth and ground her pelvis against his with deliberate intent.

Fargo chuckled soundlessly.

Jane shrugged. "I always heard that takes a man's mind off his hurts."

"Does it really work?"

"We could try it out. Then you can tell me if I've been right all these years." She raised herself slightly and slipped a hand in between them, fumbling awkwardly with Fargo's buttons until he was free of the binding cloth. Then she raised the abbreviated hem, of her dress. She wasn't wearing any underwear. Her flesh was hot against his.

Fargo tried to mount her, but the movement was

enough to send a lance of pain shooting through his head where the Comanche lance had struck him. He winced.

"Hold still," Jane whispered. "Let me."

Fargo nodded. He lay quiet, stretched out on his back, while Jane straddled him, one slim brown leg on either side of his hips. She lay on top of him like that, with his hard, erect member trapped between the flat planes of his belly and the yielding softness of hers, while she kissed and caressed him.

Then she began to wriggle, very slowly but very insistently.

"I think it's working," Fargo croaked.

Jane giggled and moved some more.

"It's definitely working," Fargo whispered.

Jane grinned. "Good. Now for the rest of the treatment." She raised her hips above him—difficult to do in the close confinement of the dirt hole where they were hiding—and he could feel the head of his cock seek and find the warm, moist opening.

With a sigh of her own pleasure, Jane slid down onto him, impaling herself on the Trailsman's lance, driving it deep inside her.

"Yeah," Fargo whispered. "It's working."

She moved her hips, slowly at first and then more quickly, grinding herself against him so that the button of her pleasure rubbed against the hard shelf of his pelvic bone. Her breath came quick and hard.

Soon the pleasure she intended to give him became pleasure she intended to take from him, and Fargo had to work just to keep up with her. He erupted with a spasm of raw, hot pleasure just as she convulsed and bucked atop him.

Both of them collapsed limply, not caring a thing about the dirt that they had dislodged from the roof of their little sanctuary and that now trickled down over their half-naked bodies.

Jane sighed and wrapped her arms tight around Fargo.

Within minutes both of them were asleep, still locked in that ultimate embrace and with her breath warm in the hollow of his throat.

"Wait here," Jane whispered. "I'm going to look around." She disentangled herself from the close, cramped position they had occupied throughout the long day and slipped out into the fresh evening air. Fargo followed close behind her.

"Skye, please, stay there."

"I'm all right. I keep telling you that. I feel much better now."

"You look awful."

"Thanks."

"You know what I meant." She blushed, probably recalling the rather large number of times they had set aside fears of discovery during the day by occupying themselves with more immediate pursuits.

"Yeah." He squeezed her hand reassuringly but continued to stand in the fresh, clean-smelling air. It was a relief to be able to stand upright again after so very many hours spent in that damned hole in the ground. It hadn't been all that hot in there, but there had been little air and no opportunity to stretch. He was thoroughly enjoying the simple act of standing on his own hind legs, able to take on whatever came.

Not that he really expected there to be any danger now. They hadn't seen or heard a Comanche since late morning when a pair of them walked the bottom of the wash, bows and war clubs held at the ready.

The Comanche had passed close enough to Fargo and Jane that they could hear the grind of their moccasins in the sand before they came into sight.

Fargo now stretched hugely, leaning backward and windmilling his arms for a moment to get his circulation back.

He really did feel much better now, despite Jane's misgivings. His head hardly hurt at all, and the pain in his ribs had receded to a dull ache. Oddly enough, it was the pair of shallow cuts on his chest that was bothering him the most, and he was not concerned about that. The cuts were clean and should heal quickly enough. For the time being they were only a minor annoyance, and soon that would be gone too.

Jane motioned him to stay where he was and crawled over the rim of the wash toward where the Comanche camp had been.

She was a damned independent female. He had to say that about her. Any normal woman would be wanting Fargo to protect her and wait on her and get her the hell out of this hostile desert. Not this one. She seemed bent on protecting him. It was a novel experience for him and one he wasn't so sure he enjoyed. He wasn't some damned invalid or some kind of pilgrim who'd go around shitting in his own blankets for fear of leaving them in the night.

Fargo shook his head and followed her.

The Comanche camp was empty, nothing more than a few patches of beaten earth and cold ashes where the fires had been. Fargo made it a point to not look at Junebug's body.

"They went south," Jane said. Apparently she was every bit as good a tracker as the Trailsman was. That was the way she had followed Fargo and how she had known it was Fargo who had run afoul of the unhorsed Comanche raiding party.

"They were heading home after they lost their horses," she told him. "Losing them was a sign of bad luck, so they had to quit the raid. Then you and that girl brought their luck back to them. So now they're going to Mexico again. That change of luck probably makes them feel invincible now." She looked darkly toward the south. "This is going to be a bloody one. That's the way they are."

She might have spent years living with the Comanche, but she certainly showed no affection for the Indians.

Fargo looked off toward the south too. If Jane was right—and he had no reason to doubt her—there were an awful lot of innocent men and women and children down to the south who would have to pay the price of the Comanche's fury. Fargo had some firsthand reasons now to think of that with sympathy for those unsuspecting families.

"You're the one who knows this country and where we can find water in it," Fargo said after a moment. "Which way do we go?" He was anxious to get to someplace, anyplace, where he could replace his horse and guns and get on Calder's trail again.

"You're really feeling better, Skye?"

"Uh huh."

"Do you feel up to getting back at those Comanche?"

Fargo raised an eyebrow and looked at the butcher knife that was once again tucked behind the cord that served her as a belt. They'd had to remove it for a while because of the obvious dangers while they were whiling away the day. If this crazy damn female intended to jump a war party of Comanche with nothing but one knife between them . . .

She looked at him and guessed what he was thinking. "No, silly. But I do have an idea."

"Yes?"

"There's a stage station twenty, maybe thirty miles south of here. We—they, I mean—used to attack it nearly every time they came this way. It was almost like a game for them, it was always so easy. I'd bet they'll attack it again tomorrow morning. They spent most of today looking for us. Tonight they'll rest up and celebrate their luck returning. Tomorrow morning they'll want to show off that new luck by attacking the stage station."

"That's right," Fargo said. "And if I'm understanding you correctly, what you want to do is make a fast walk south tonight so we can be there when the Comanche jump that relay station tomorrow morning."

Jane smiled at him. "Yep. The company should have some guns there. And this year they'd be warned. There would be at least three, maybe four of us to fight."

"Bloodthirsty wench, aren't you?" Fargo asked.

"I had good teachers," she said seriously.

"Thirty miles?"

She nodded. "More or less."

He grinned. "Hell, woman, we can make that by midnight."

"They'll have food there too."

"I could stand some of that."

"If I go too fast for you, let me know," Jane said.

"That'll be the damn day . . ."

But Jane wasn't listening to him any longer. She had already started off in a long-striding swing toward the south.

Damned if the Trailsman didn't have to hustle to keep up with her.

Fargo's crack about getting there by midnight had been just a bit optimistic. It was closer to three-thirty in the morning before they arrived at the tiny, isolated relay station. The place consisted of a low adobe building, a set of corrals, a well, and the burnt-out remains of a daub-and-wattle barn.

"Looks like things've changed since you were here last," he said as they walked the last few yards to the place. He pointed. The corrals held about a dozen head of horses. More than enough to please the shit out of a bunch of raiding Comanches.

"That's asking for trouble," Jane said. She was still going strong after all the walking. And she had damn sure impressed Fargo with her pathfinding. She had brought them right to the station without any wasted steps. She had learned well when she was with the Comanche.

They stopped at the well for a long, welcome drink, and Fargo refilled the canteen even before they approached the station itself. He had learned a few things through the years too, and one of them was to make no assumptions about coming opportunities. A chance skipped might well be a chance lost, whether the subject was refilling a canteen or reloading a revolver.

"Come on," he said. He was tired and his head was hurting again, a low, dull throbbing that wasn't particularly bad at any given moment but that wouldn't quit now that it had returned. "We need to make sure there're some guns here or get the hell out while we can."

He pulled the latch string on the heavy door and went inside without knocking.

Their greeting was unexpected.

Without warning, half a dozen gun muzzles yawned out of the shadows, every one of the things pointed squarely at them, and the sound of half a dozen hammers being drawn to full cock followed quickly behind.

Fargo froze into position at the open door so quickly that Jane bumped into his back and almost knocked him down.

"I think they got guns here," Fargo said dryly over his shoulder.

"Skye? Skye Fargo? Is that you, you son of a bitch? What the fuck are you doin' here? Somebody light that lamp, dammit."

A match flared, and Fargo could see Jim Nelson and his troop of rangers bedded on the floor of the station. Behind them was a blinking, sleepy-eyed civilian on a regular bed—had to be the stationmaster, Fargo figured—who wasn't yet awake enough to know what was going on.

The same light that showed Fargo who they had blundered into also showed Jim Nelson that there was a woman with the Trailsman.

"Jesus God!" Nelson blurted when he saw Jane. "I'm sorry 'bout my language, ma'am. Honest I am."

142

The rangers let down the hammers of their Colts and tucked them out of sight. Most of the boys were only partially dressed and looked uncomfortable with Jane in the room.

"So what're you doing here, Skye?" Nelson asked in a more polite tone.

Fargo explained, and the men looked at Jane with respect.

By the time Fargo and Jane were done talking, Nelson and his boys were grinning.

"Come dawn, eh?" Nelson asked. "I wouldn't be surprised at that." He shook his head. "Thought we'd put a crimp in those bastards' tails—beggin' your pardon, ma'am—when we cleaned out their horse herd a while back. Didn't worry so much about losing them after that. Hard to track a man afoot in this country, you know. But now if they got horses again . . ."

"Where do you have their herd stashed, Jim?" Fargo asked. "That sure isn't the whole bunch out there in the corral."

"Naw," Nelson said with a wave of his hand. "Most of them weren't worth keepin' anyhow. We shot the most of them to make sure the Comanch' couldn't get them back. Those are just our horses and a few keepers outta the bunch." Nelson fingered his chin for a moment, then grinned again. "I got an idea, Skye. Ma'am, would you mind turning your back for a minute while my boys get themselves decent? I think we got us some work t' do."

It was crowded and smelly inside the low adobe. In addition to eight men and one woman, the building housed ten horses. The horses were no happier to be there than the men were to have them as close company, but now the only animals out in the corral were the single relay change belonging to the stage company. The Comanches wouldn't find anything amiss when they attacked the place at dawn.

"Sure wish you'd rebuilt that damn barn, Ez," Nelson said at one point. He wrinkled his nose as a stocky chestnut passed wind behind his back.

"No point," the stationmaster said. "The bastards never let it stand long enough t' be worthwhile rebuildin'. Got so's I could count on 'em. They'd stop in once, twice a year an' relieve me of whatever horses I had an' burn the barn an' send a few arrers my way just to keep me from gettin' cocky. They quit bein' serious about tryin' to kill me, though." He grinned and spat a stream of yellow tobacco juice onto the already fouled floor. "Got me one o' them newfangled Henry repeaters, an' I was pickin' off too many of them. You could almost say we come to an agreement on the subject."

"I hope you ain't gonna mind if we mess up your arrangement with 'em," Nelson said.

"Huh. You won't find me cryin'. Had me a woman here for a while, you know. The Comanch' got to 'er early last season. Made me mad, they did. She was a pretty good ol' woman."

The stationmaster hefted his long-barreled Henry and grinned. He shot another stream of tobacco juice onto the floor, dribbling some of it into his beard.

Fargo checked the loads in the Colts the rangers had given him. That was one good thing about those boys. They always had firearms to spare, it seemed.

But he had had to take some teasing from Nelson and his men in order to get his hands on these weapons.

"You want more, boy?" Nelson had asked. "We know how you are 'bout losing the damn things. Gave you one good Walker a'ready, and what'd you do with the damn thing? Gave it to some Comanch', that's what." Nelson turned and winked at his men, and every damned one of them had laughed. It would have been enough to irritate a man if it hadn't been said in good humor.

"An' how come you haven't told us how much hair you raised when you was losin' your guns, Skye?" another ranger asked.

"Hush up and watch out the window," Fargo said, turning his back and peering through a loophole cut into the thick adobe wall. That particular subject was one he didn't want to get into right now. He was feeling a bit sore on the point.

Jane was at the loophole next to his. The rangers had given her a brace of revolvers and a double-barreled shotgun without hesitation. Apparently they were not so old-fashioned about the supposed delicacy of ladies that they were going to turn down her offer of assistance.

The false dawn was already making the sky grow pale. The sage and low-growing mesquite outside was still starkly black and colorless, though. The sun wouldn't be long in coming now.

"When do you figure?" Fargo asked. Jane would be even more familiar with the Comanche habits than Nelson and his boys. And they were no slouches at their jobs.

"When the sun is half over the horizon. The first group will come straight out of it. They'll already be out there waiting on it."

"Remember," Nelson said. "Wait until they reach the gate." He seemed eager, and so did his men.

Fargo remembered now how close Nelson liked to get before he engaged the enemy. The man simply had no nerves—or didn't show them, if he did have any.

A horse stamped and shifted, disturbed the animal standing next to him, and within moments the inside of the station was a mass of churning hooves and moving bodies.

"Whoa, dammit, whoa."

The men gentled the unhappy horses, and quiet returned, the horses standing patiently with their heads down. The rangers bent to the firing ports in the walls with their guns ready.

Maybe, Fargo thought, those horses knew something that the rest of them didn't.

Minutes later the Comanche came riding in like they were having fun, not like it was a real raid at all.

They were riding loose and easy. They yipped and

yelped and hollered and waved their lances in the air—a weapon that Fargo had increasing respect for—and acted in general like a bunch of kids on holiday. This was routine old stuff for them.

Fargo noticed that those few who had rifles or pistols were not firing them. He knew damn good and well that some of them had revolvers, because they had his. They waved them in the air but didn't waste their precious ammunition on this little celebratory raid.

Fargo recognized the kid who had stopped by for a chat and a friendly kick or several. Damn him. The boy wasn't much for size, but he was hell for mean. It graveled Fargo to have to let him ride past in that first yelping sweep.

The Comanche charged out of the sun, raced through the yard in front of the station, and whirled back toward the corral where the big, heavy-bodied draft horses were beginning to get nervous.

"Now," Jim Nelson said softly as the first of them leaned down for the gate latch.

A sheet of flame erupted from the firing ports on that side of the adobe building, and four of the Comanche toppled off their horses. At least one of them was done for. The others may have been only wounded.

The timbre of the Comanche yelling changed. They weren't having fun any longer. Some of them sounded scared.

"Pour it on 'em, boys."

The boys did, emptying their first revolvers in a thunder-roll of noise and smoke. And emptying the backs of a good number of Comanche ponies too.

"That's it, boys."

It wasn't only the boys who were doing the firing, though. Jane was cutting down on the Comanche hot and heavy, firing almost as fast as she could work hammer and trigger on her borrowed revolvers, not really taking the time for careful aim but letting the shots rip in a flurry of hate and revenge.

"That's it, boys. Now close on 'em."

Nelson threw the bar off the heavy door and shoved, letting light and a welcome drift of fresh air into the place. He and most of his rangers ran out into the yard with a roar. The stationmaster, Ez, remained prudently behind, keeping the horses from following the men outside, where they were apt to be snatched away by the Indians.

Jane beat Fargo to the door and ran through it with every bit as much determination as the rangers were showing. She had discarded her empty revolvers and was carrying the shotgun one of the men had given her.

The Comanches were getting themselves organized now—as organized as they were likely to get, anyway. An Indian's fighting style rides on flash and glory, not discipline.

Two of the painted, half-naked warriors made an assault on the corral gate. They had come for the horses, and by damn, it was horses they were after. Nelson and his men cut them down, knocking them off their ponies into the dust of the station yard.

A trio charged around the back end of the station and into the yard behind Nelson's men. Fargo shot one, his slug taking the man in the willow-and-quill breastplate he was wearing and sending splinters and blood flying.

Beside Fargo, Jane fired one barrel of the shotgun. The charge of heavy pellets wiped away the top half of a Comanche's face. She loosed the other barrel at the third Indian but fired too high and missed. Fargo took aim, led the fast-moving target, and spilled the Comanche off his pony with a shot that took the Indian low in the side.

Another Comanche came seemingly out of nowhere to ram his horse between Fargo and Jane, the off shoulder of the running animal catching Jane in the back and flinging her to the ground. The Comanche had a war club hanging from a thong on his wrist, but he was ignoring the weapon for the moment. He bent low and at full gallop reached down to grab his wounded comrade and throw him onto the pony's rump behind him as he lined out for the safety of distance.

Fargo took aim and shot the wounded Comanche again before the two of them got out of range. It wasn't a sporting shot, but then, this wasn't a sport they were engaged in. A live, recovered Comanche was a menace.

The twice-wounded Comanche fell to the ground again. This time he lay facedown and unmoving. The Indian who had rescued him once took one look behind him and wheeled out of sight around the side of the station building. There was some more shooting over there, so apparently Ez was still in the scrap.

Jim Nelson called out, "Duck, Skye," and fired both revolvers from the hip at something behind Fargo.

Fargo ducked, and the heavy wooden shaft of a lance sliced through the air above him while a few yards away a Comanche thumped into the dirt with two bullets in his chest.

The Indian was bleeding and wheezing and obviously dying, but he wasn't done fighting. He pulled his knife and began to crawl toward Nelson, who was concentrating on reloading his guns.

Fargo walked over to the dying Comanche and finished him with a bullet to the back of his head. It wasn't until after he shot him that Fargo realized the dead Comanche was the kid who liked to kick captive whites.

"Jane," Fargo screamed.

A Comanche, the same one who had made that rescue attempt a few minutes earlier, Fargo thought, but carrying a lance now that he had picked up somewhere, came racing around from behind the station. The Indian seemed intent on driving straight for Jane and no one else. Surely, Fargo thought, he couldn't be so interested in taking a woman as all that.

But he was.

He ducked as one of the rangers fired a revolver into his face, and he gave the young ranger a kick in the face as he charged past, knocking the youngster to the ground. It would have been easy coup for the Comanche, but he continued to head for Jane.

Fargo's Colt leapt into position. He took aim, using precious seconds to make sure of the target, and squeezed.

The hammer clinked dully on a spent cap. The damned gun was empty.

"Behind you, Jane. Down!"

Instead of dropping, Jane spun. She lifted her shotgun and earred back both hammers.

"No!"

Her damn gun was empty too. Fargo remembered that even if she didn't.

She was still standing like that, grimly sighting over the barrels of an empty shotgun, cocking and snapping the hammers over and over, seeming not even to realize that the gun wasn't shooting, when the Comanche's lance tip ripped through her belly and emerged a red and bloody six or eight inches past her back.

The Comanche dropped his hold on the lance and raised his face and fists toward the sky with a yammering, ululating war whoop.

Fargo leapt for the Indian. He grabbed the war club that still hung suspended from his wrist, pulled and twisted.

The Comanche was dragged off the horse's back, and Fargo was onto him with feet and teeth and bare hands.

The Indian tried to fight back, but Fargo was enraged, capable of seeing or comprehending nothing but the enemy who was beneath him.

There was a knife at Fargo's belt, but he didn't take time for it, didn't have the time or sense to give it thought.

Blinded by his rage, the Trailsman clutched the painted warrior by the braids on the sides of his head and used them as handles while he beat the struggling Comanche's brains out on a rock.

"Skye. Hey, Skye. You wanta stop now?"

Fargo blinked, feeling like he was just waking out of a deep sleep, and looked around.

Jim Nelson and his boys were standing around, slouching, slowly reloading emptied firearms. There wasn't a Comanche in sight, althought the corral held some horses that Fargo remembered but that hadn't been there a while ago. Nelson was packing his jaw with cut tobacco.

"Yeah?" Fargo asked.

Nelson shrugged. "Thought you might wanta slow down for a spell. You know. Rest. Have some breakfast. You can come back an' finish the job later, if you want."

"What job?"

Nelson acted like he was amused.

Fargo looked down.

The face of a dead Comanche peered sightlessly up at him, pale and bloodless now under the hideous paint. His thick braids were wrapped tight in Fargo's aching fists, and there was blood all over the ground, his head, and Fargo's hands and chests. It had splattered quite a lot.

Fargo let the head drop limply back to the earth, releasing his grip finally. The bone and brain that had been at the back of the dead Comanche's skull had been turned into mush by the battering.

Fargo shivered and came slowly to his feet. He was weak-kneed and felt like puking. "Have I been gone long?"

"A spell," Nelson conceded. "Happens sometimes." He shifted his chew to the other side of his jaw and spat. The juice did not yet have good color and he worked on it with his teeth for a bit.

"Yeah," Fargo said. He swayed a little as he stood. He didn't think he'd ever been so tired before. Never. He felt utterly drained.

"You'd best come inside, Skye. Need some help?"

Fargo shook his head. "I can manage." He did, but it took a major effort of will to walk from the yard into the station without falling on his face.

Ez had a fire going in the stove and was cooking something that smelled like manna and would be even more welcome.

Jane was laid out on Ez's bed, with a scrap of tarp under her to keep from getting blood onto the station-master's blankets. The lance hadn't been removed from her body, but at least it had been broken off front and rear so she could be laid flat. She was still alive and completely aware of what was going on around her.

"I got him, didn't I, Skye?" Her voice was weak, but she sounded satisfied.

"You sure did, honey," Fargo lied. "You got him."

"Good." Her face twisted in a spasm of pain.

"Is there anything I can do for you?"

"Naw." She smiled. "Just so I got Arthur. That's what matters."

"Arthur?"

"That was his white name." Her voice was becoming weaker now. Slower. "Long time ago."

"I didn't know . . ."

"He was a stinkin' Comanch', Skye. Was for a long time.' She tried to smile. "I killed the son of a bitch, though, didn' I?"

"You sure did, honey."

Her lips twisted and she cried out. She was fading rapidly.

Fargo sat carefully on the side of the bed and smoothed her hair back from her forehead. There was nothing he could do to help her. They both knew that. He wished that wasn't so.

"Two Scalps," she said.

"What, honey?" He took a corner of Ez's blanket and wiped the sweat and grime off her forehead and cheeks.

"Called himself Two Scalps. Comanch' name. No more Arthur." She looked like she was going to cry.

"You got him, honey," he lied again.

"Good!" She spat the word out with unexpected force. "Son of a bitch." A tear trickled out of the corner of one eye and rolled down her cheek. Fargo petted her again.

"Used to be my brother." The words came out in a whisper. They were the last she spoke, although once before she went, she raised her hand and fumbled with it for Fargo's. He clasped her hand in his and she squeezed. She had little strength left. A sparrow could have squeezed harder than that.

Then she was gone.

Fargo sat beside her for a moment. But there was no point in that.

Dammit!

Fargo stood with a sigh.

"Best get you some breakfast, Skye." Jim Nelson and his boys were at the long table that served stagecoach passengers. "You comin' with us, Skye?"

"Where you bound now, Jim?"

"Aw, chasin' them damn Comanch' some more, I reckon. We got most of those horses back, but they still got a few. Wanta make sure they're headed home for sure this time. And pick a few more of 'em off if we get the chance. You comin'?"

"Only if you need me mighty bad. I owe you."

"Bullshit. We owed you first." Nelson grinned at him around a mouthful of fried mush.

"We got your guns back, Mr. Fargo," the young ranger said. The kid looked no worse for the wear he had gotten when Arthur Two Scalps kicked him.

Fargo nodded. He felt disjointed, like he wasn't really part of the world the rest of humanity inhabited. Not right now, anyway. "Thanks."

"There's spare horses an' shit," Nelson said. "We can get you outfitted."

"Thanks," Fargo mumbled again.

"You still figure to go after them boys from back in San Antone?"

"Yeah."

"Wish we could help you, but . . ."

"I know."

"Look, Skye . . . I'm sorry about the young lady. You know?"

"I know, Jim." Fargo had never felt so weary in his life. Drained. Drained and used up, somewhere down deep in his soul. "I know." He dropped into a chair at the table and stared without interest at the food that Ez put before him. Jane had never told him where Calder was going.

As he rode away from the station and Nelson and his boys, Fargo was bothered by thoughts of loss. He had been with Jane . . . what? Three nights and a day? Day and a half? Something like that. It seemed longer. He missed her as he rode north toward the last place he knew Calder and his men had been. Back where the Comanche had interrupted things for him and Junebug.

Losing women seemed to be becoming a habit. It was a habit he would rather break. He missed Jane. Junebug too, for that matter, if in a different way. He had felt responsible for both of them.

It was easier riding than it had been walking. He found the place with ease. The carrion-eaters led him to it. He knew why they were there and ignored them. Some things were best left alone.

He turned west again, following the trail Calder had left.

Time had passed, obscuring some of the marks left by the passage of the three horses. And now, with the herd of loose stock no longer with Calder's party, there was less for Fargo to follow. But there was enough.

Fargo wanted the Ovaro back.

Even more now, he wanted the man known as Calder to pay for the agonies he had caused. The Trailsman would have found a way to track a sparrow through a sandstorm if that was what it took to reach Calder.

He rode steadily west, alone on the dry, ugly south plains. Searching. Constantly aware of his surroundings. If the Comanche had stumbled onto him again, it would have been their bad luck. The mood he was in now was hardly pleasant.

11

Skye Fargo stood for a moment, light-headed, weaving on rubbery knees. The horse he had been leading for the past day and a half pushed past him, stumbled down the bank, and walked out into the shallow river. It was in even worse shape than Fargo, although it had been receiving most of the little water he had carried. It buried its muzzle in the flow of sun-warmed, alkaline water and drank deep, its ears working back and forth like a pair of pump handles as it swallowed.

Fargo gave it only a few moments, then followed. He walked out into the Pecos, raised a handful of the bitter but lifegiving water to his cracked lips, then led the horse out onto the western bank. Too much water too soon and the animal would founder. Fargo tied it there, then turned back to lie immersed in the tepid, flowing water, soaking moisture into his pores, turning his head now and then to drink, wallowing in the good feel of it.

Soon he would let the horse drink again. Refill the canteens. Then he would move on again.

He looked grimly toward the west.

Calder. The son of a bitch had fouled the last two tanks Fargo had found. The water had been unfit for use by man or animal.

Calder had to figure he'd finally eluded any last remaining pursuit with that trick. He was fouling the water just for spite.

Fargo had gotten the horse through on the strength of a few stunted prickly pears with the spiny thorns burnt off the soft, moist, pulpy hands so the horse could get nourishment and a hint of water from them.

Fargo had made it through on less than that: raw determination and the blood of an unwary coyote that had approached his camp in the thin light of the predawn.

Skye Fargo had survived. The man known as Calder would not.

Fargo let the horse drink again. Then he tugged his cinches tight and mounted the horse. Calder was ahead. But not far enough. There wasn't enough country between Mexico and Canada to keep Fargo from finding the man.

"Hello." Fargo nodded and sat on the tired horse, waiting politely for permission to dismount.

"Suh," the sentry barked. The infantry private stood rigidly at attention, eyes correctly forward and long-barreled, muzzle-loading Springfield upright at his side. His wool blouse was buttoned to the neck and stained dark with sweat. He looked like he might pass out from the heat without warning.

"Is there . . . Never mind." Behind the lone sentry, Fargo could see a heavier, older man approaching from the shade of the guard hut. This one wore the same heavy woolen uniform, but his collar was unbuttoned and a set of chevrons showed bright yellow on his sleeves. The sergeant of the guard, most likely.

Behind the guard hut was the bustle and activity of Fort Union, the army's primary resupply point for the entire Southwest. It wasn't a fort out of a storybook illustration, with high walls and battlements and watch-towers, but the real thing. A collection of low-roofed, sunbaked buildings that looked like warehouses. Most of them probably were warehouses. Wagons, mules, soldiers in undress fatigues, and swearing civilian teamsters moved busily back and forth through the many buildings.

"Suh," the sentry barked again when the sergeant reached them. "Guard post number one wishes to report, suh."

"Dry up, Pearsall," the sergeant said in a gravelly voice. "I can see what guard post number one wishes to report."

"Yes, *suh*," the sentry snapped.

The sergeant gave Fargo a shrug that might have been an apology and ignored the rigidly officious sentry while he dragged a plug of tobacco out of his pocket, bit off a chew, and offered the evil-looking plug to Fargo. Fargo declined.

"What can we do for you, mister?"

"I'm looking for some friends of mine. Three men."

"Sojers, are they?"

"No. Civilians. They're on horseback. They started out a few days ahead of me, and we were supposed to meet here." It seemed a plausible-enough lie. Of course, there might be some objection by the military if a lone civilian walked in and gunned down three men in the middle of an army post. But the hell with it. Fargo would worry about that when the time came. The first order of business would be to find and gun down those three civilian sons of bitches.

The sergeant shook his head and sighed. "I wisht you damn drifters wouldn't do that."

"Do what, Sergeant?"

"Wouldn't go thinking Union was some kind of damn hotel or whatever you seem to think it is. Every son of a biscuit-eater who comes acrost the damn Santa Fe Trail thinks ol' Union is the place for meetings or laying up or whatever. We got no time for all that, mister. No time for you. Your friends ain't here."

"But they said—"

"Don't care what they said." The sergeant spat into the dust close to the rigid sentry's polished black brogans.

Fargo got the impression that the sentry was a by-the-book little asshole and not necessarily popular with his superiors. He likely figured to take the stripes off some-one else's arm and put them on his own sleeves.

"We try to tell people, but nobody listens. This ain't one of them posts like up North where they let anybody do whatever they want. Here if you ain't got business with th' army, you ain't got permission to come onta the post. You got business with th' army, mister?"

"No. I already told you I'm here expecting to meet some friends, and—"

"You ain't got official business, you ain't coming onto post. Private Pearsall here wouldn't like it. An' I know you don't wanta rile Private Pearsall." He winked at Fargo. The man was doing his job, but he was trying not to be unpleasant about it.

"Any idea where my friends might be?" Fargo had lost the tracks of the men in all the disruptions caused by wagon traffic on the nearby Santa Fe Trail. The two forks of the busy trail, the original route through Raton Pass, and the dry but shorter Cimarron Cutoff, joined close to Fort Union. Santa Fe itself was still a good distance away, on the far side of the Sangre de Cristo Mountains, which loomed high and jagged to the west.

"Not here," the sergeant said. "Likely Las Vegas. If your friends stopped here, they'll have got chased off just like you are. Try Vegas. It's only a little ways south o' here on the trail."

Fargo smiled. The sergeant and his rules about civil-ians at the fort solved a problem for him. Getting crossways with the military about killing civilians on an army post wouldn't have been ideal. Now he knew that Calder was not at Union. He was pleased.

"Thank you, Sergeant." Fargo touched a finger to the brim of his hat and turned the horse away from guard post number one.

He was close now. He could feel it. Calder and his two men were almost within his grasp.

They were here in Las Vegas. Fargo found the Ovaro in one of the several large corrals on the north edge of the town. The big pinto came to the rail, whuffing softly through its velvety nostrils, and submitted to the scratching Fargo gave it in the sensitive hollow under its jaw.

The horse had been hard-used since Fargo saw it last. There was the beginning of a saddle sore just behind its withers. Calder had been careless with it. That alone would have been enough to enrage Fargo. Not that he needed anything more.

"Something you want, mister?" a voice asked suspiciously from behind him.

Fargo turned. The hostler was gray-haired and half-crippled from old injuries. There was no way the man could know that the horse had been stolen. And no proof Fargo could give him at the moment. Any claims the Trailsman made here and now would just be so many unsubstantiated words.

"I'm looking for the men who came in with this animal," he said. He wanted to say more, but there would have been no point.

The hostler grunted. "You can see they ain't here."

"Yeah. Thanks." Fargo turned away, leaving the Ovaro standing on the other side of the corral rails. He headed for town.

Las Vegas was bigger than he had expected, and undoubtedly bigger than it had been before Fort Union was established north of it.

There was a small nucleus of adobe buildings, surrounded now by other, newer structures, many of them saloons, to cater to the needs of the heavy traffic on the Santa Fe Trail and of the soldiers and civilian freighters who had business at the fort.

A complex of corrals and wagon parks lay on the north side of the town, nearest the army post. Beyond those were dozens of hole-in-the-wall dance halls and whorehouses.

There was probably a respectable section of town too, but Fargo couldn't see it from the corrals.

He left the horse Jim Nelson had given him, tied to a rail near the patient Ovaro, and walked into town.

His Colt was loose in his holster and he carried a second revolver behind his belt.

There was no sense in asking after strangers here. Ninety percent of the men in town would be strangers passing through or would be off-duty soldiers who would neither know nor care anything about the civilians on the streets. Fargo would have to hunt them out for himself.

At least he had the advantage of having seen them on the street back in San Antonio. He remembered Calder and each of the bastard's men. They had seen him only at a distance.

Not that he gave a crap if they recognized him or not. In fact, it would make things easier if they would try to gun him on sight. No one would object to a man defending himself.

The Trailsman paused at the doorway of the first saloon he came to. Calder might be inside there, only a few feet away.

On the other hand . . .

Dammit. He had to do this by logic, not emotion. The way that spit-and polish private back at Union would have done. He had a job to do here, and he didn't want anyone interfering when he claimed the Ovaro and the bank loot Calder and his men were carrying.

He walked on past the saloon doorway, hung with strings of brightly colored fly beads, and went in search of the local sheriff.

The man was in his office, sitting behind the bare top of a scarred desk with his boots propped up on the edge of a partially opened drawer. Fargo introduced himself and stated his business. The sheriff, a man named Hansen, listened without comment until Fargo was done.

"You have a warrant?" the sheriff asked. He sounded bored.

"No. I already explained that I—"

"You don't have a warrant," Hansen said.

"I don't have a warrant for their arrest," Fargo agreed.

Hansen pulled his top desk drawer open a few inches, fumbled inside it for a cigar, and proceeded to light the foul-smelling thing. "Let me get this straight then, mister. You come in here off the street, a fella I've never seen before, and you tell me you want to arrest some men who you say allegedly committed this crime all the way over in the middle of Texas. And you say you've been authorized to recover this here horse and money and take them back to Texas. But you don't have any kind of a warrant nor authorization from anybody. But you say that I should believe you because it's so. Am I getting this right, mister? Is that what you say?"

"That's right," Fargo said mildly. Hansen hadn't invited him to sit, but Fargo helped himself to a chair anyway and propped his boot heels up on Hansen's desk.

The sheriff eyed Fargo's boots for a moment, then said, "You do push a fella, don't you?"

"That's what you say," Fargo said in a soft voice. "I came in here trying to do things right. I thought you should know what was going on before I went and braced those boys. You're welcome to check what I say. Send a wire to banker Harry Burton in San Antonio. He'll confirm what I told you."

Hansen snorted. "That's an easy kind of lie, mister. There's no telegraph connection from here all the way to Texas."

"I saw the poles and wires, Sheriff. Surely—"

Hansen grunted. "Government line. It runs from Union to Santa Fe, down to the territorial capital. That's all the farther it goes, which you probably knew already anyhow."

"Look, Sheriff Hansen, I don't know why you're dragging your heels on this thing. I'm just trying to—"

"Don't you go accusing me of that shit, mister," the sheriff snapped. "Whatever you're thinking, you just forget it. You hear me?" Hansen dropped his feet to the floor with a crash and sat forward in his chair, the cigar jammed between his teeth so tightly that he almost bit through the end of the thing. He looked furious. "You can't come into my office and make wild accusations, mister. Not about me nor anybody else in this town. And you'd best get that through your lying head. You hear me?"

Fargo had struck a nerve somewhere, although he didn't know how or what. That damn sure hadn't been his intention.

Unless Calder and his boys hadn't been coming to Las Vegas as just a stopping place where they could let down and spend some of their loot.

Had those boys been coming home when they stopped here?

That might explain Hansen's reaction.

Hansen grabbed the cigar out of his jaw and stabbed it toward Fargo like a weapon. "You better think mighty hard before you spread any lies around this town, mister. You keep up with that kind of shit, and I'll have you in my jail so fast you won't know what direction you're pointed until there's steel bars all around you. D'you understand me, mister?"

Fargo smiled at him. "I believe I do, Sheriff. I believe that I do now. And I thank you for all the information you've given me." He stood, Hansen continuing to glare up at him from the sheriff's seat behind his desk.

"I want you out of my town before night falls, mister. And don't be coming back again. You hear?"

Fargo didn't answer. By then he had reached the door and was out on the street in front of the sheriff's office. He could hear Hansen blustering and threatening behind him, but he paid no attention to the man.

Damned interesting, he thought.

He was glad he had decided to stop by and see the fool, though. It gave him a better idea of what he would be up against here. Much better.

Fargo had only a few minutes to wait. He was leaning against the corner of a building a block down from the jail and across the street. He looked for all the world like a loafer idling the afternoon away, but his eyes were alert beneath the brim of his hat.

There was no sense in conducting a long search if he had someone to lead him to where he wanted to go.

And he damn sure thought he did.

Sure enough, a very little while after Fargo left the sheriff's office, Sheriff Hansen appeared on the sidewalk with a hat on his head and the cigar between his teeth.

Hansen looked up and down the street, failed to spot Fargo anywhere, and hurried off toward the south end of town, away from the saloon district.

Fargo left his position in the shade beside the greengrocer's and ambled along behind the sheriff, keeping close to the store fronts he passed so he could duck out of sight if need be. But Hansen seemed to think he was in the clear now. He didn't once look back over his shoulder.

Passersby on the street greeted Hansen. The sheriff nodded curtly and hurried on. He was a worried man.

Interesting, Fargo thought. He checked to make sure the Colt was free in his holster and continued to follow Sheriff Hansen.

The man reached the end of the business district. Off to the right were some handsome houses. Fargo had found the respectable part of Las Vegas. There were tree-shaded streets and nicely tended yards there.

Instead of going toward them, though, Hansen turned left. Fargo increased his stride, not wanting to lose sight of the man he was following.

Hansen broke into a shuffling trot once he was away

from the main street. He moved awkwardly, like he was already tiring. Out of shape, Fargo thought, and in a hurry.

The sheriff took a narrow footpath that led toward a collection of sagging adobes and daub-and-wattle shacks. Scruffy chickens and naked children shared the litter and the dust of the ground between the shacks. Fargo slowed his pace, allowing Sheriff Hansen to get farther ahead of him. He would be too easily spotted here.

Hansen skirted a pigsty where half a dozen unhealthy-looking shoats were panting in their unshaded confinement, glanced once behind him without spotting Fargo, and hurried on to the last of the jacales. There were no windows in the shack. A tattered blanket had been hung over the doorway but was pushed aside now and held open with a stick pushed between the vertical poles where some of the mud plaster had flaked away.

Fancy, Fargo thought. He increased his pace again and slipped up to the side of the shack.

Inside it he could hear Hansen's voice, strained and panting from the exertion of the walk. The man hadn't looked in that bad a condition, but then maybe he had something wrong with his lungs.

"You dumb sons of bitches," Hansen was saying. "He's here."

"Who's here?" It was a voice Fargo had never heard before. But he'd have been willing to bet that the unfamiliar voice came from a face he would have recognized.

"Some guy who's been following you dumb fucks all the way from Texas, that's who."

"Come on, Arnie. Nobody followed us. Nobody could've."

"Yeah. We made sure o' that," another voice put in.

Fargo leaned against the side of the jacale, carefully lest the rickety thing fall down from his weight against it. He smiled to himself. Right. Nobody'd followed. They had made sure of that. Sure they had.

"I'm telling you, there's a guy here who says you stole his damn horse. He's come to take it back. And you and that money you stole too, dammit. I'm telling you, he's here."

There was silence for a moment. Then someone said, "Sure wouldn't'a believed that, Arnie."

"Ah, hell. You can fix it for us, Arnie."

"You always have," another said.

"If you had to steal a damn horse," Hansen said, "you could've stolen one that belonged to a pilgrim." There was a note of complaint in the sheriff's tone.

"Jesus, Arnie, we didn't stop to ask permission."

"No way we coulda known whose horse it was, Arnie. An' ole Billy's horse got shot out from under him."

"We was away clean until that happened."

"You fools," Hansen moaned.

"You can square it, Arnie."

"Just run the guy off. Or tell him you'll arrest us or something."

"Hell, that'll satisfy him."

"I'll tell you what will satisfy this man," Hansen said. "Your blood, that's what will satisfy this one. I could see it in his eyes. This guy figures to shoot you down. Every one of you. Or take you back to San Antonio. That would be even worse."

"So take care of it. Damn, Arnie. What's the big deal this time? It isn't like you've ever worried about it before."

Arnie Hansen groaned out loud. "You just don't get it, do you? Do you know who the guy is? Well, do you?"

"What difference does that make?" someone whined.

"I'll tell you what difference it makes this time, damn you. I didn't let on when the guy was talking to me. But the guy's name is Fargo. Skye Fargo. Have you dumb bastards ever hear of him?"

There was a moment of silence, then one of them said, "The one they call the Trailsman?"

"Yeah. That one."

"So the guy's got a reputation. So what? You can square it, Arnie."

"Not this time. I'm not so sure I can this time. You didn't see the guy. I did."

"You square it, Arnie, or we'll take care of it ourselves." There was a snort of laughter and the sound of a revolver hammer being cocked.

"Dammit, not around here. You know that. I can't have any trouble around here, or you know what people will say. If anybody thinks I'm favoring my own, they'd throw me out of office. You know they would. Probably wouldn't even wait till the next election. They'd have me out before I could spit."

"Well, we ain't gonna let anybody take us, Arnie. No way."

"Don't you push me too far, Wiley. I'm not going to put my job on the line for you boys. Not with that kind of thing around here, I won't. What you do in somebody else's jurisdiction is their problem. But I'm not going to lose my job for you."

Fargo damn near burst out laughing. Once the chickens came home to roost, it looked like it was every bird for himself. Assholes.

"Then you fix it, Arnie."

"Tell this guy whatever it takes to make him turn around. Send him back to Texas. You fix it, or we'll take care of it ourselves."

"Hell, Arnie, I don't care what kinda reputation this Trailsman guy has, he can't stand up to all three of us."

"Four of us," another voice said.

"Three," Hansen corrected. He sounded very upset.

"Okay, three. Hell, Arnie, we ain't scared of him."

"You ought to be." There was a pause. "Look, maybe if I turn the horse over to him, promise him I'll arrest you and send you back for trial. Better yet, I will arrest you. Put you in the jail. Just for a little while, though. I can impound the horse and the money. Give him back his horse and tell him I'll send the money back to that bank by a draft. Then, as soon as he's gone, I can turn you loose again. No harm done. Why, that way I could even look pretty good to the voters. You know? Dealing fair, even putting my own kin behind bars. Until it turns out that the charges weren't valid. But it'd look good to the voters. And I can square it with everybody, about how it was all a mistake, soon as this Fargo guy is out of town."

"I don't wanta spend any time in your damn jail, Arnie. Not me."

"It won't be but a day or so. It won't hurt you any, for God's sake. And it'll get you out of this jam."

"I don't know, Arnie. I kinda favor that horse Billy took. Helluva good animal."

"Do you want to take a chance on going to jail for real, or worse, just so you can keep that horse?"

"No, but—"

"Dammit. If you want me to fix this for you, you got to go along with me on it. You got to let me handle it. Surely even you aren't so damn stupid that you can't see that. And you won't be behind bars long, just enough for me to get that Fargo out of the way. Then I'll explain everything to the folks around here and turn you loose. It'll all be forgotten before the weekend."

"I don't know . . ."

"You either do it or I wash my hands of this mess and of you too. Now I mean it this time, boys. I really mean it this time."

Someone laughed. That was a threat they must have heard before.

"I mean it," Hansen insisted.

"Give us some time to think it over, Arnie."

"You don't have any time to think about it. Once that guy starts asking questions, he's going to come up with you three right off. We got to do this right now. I'll take you over to the jail and put you behind the bars right now. Then the guy can't touch you. I'll give him his horse back and send him on his way. Hell, he ought to be out of here by morning. And tomorrow afternoon you boys will be back on the street, just as easy as you please. Now bring that money out from wherever you hid it and give it to me."

"Now wait a minute, Arnie . . ."

"Dammit. I'll give it back to you tomorrow. Soon as that Fargo leaves town. I'll give it back when I let you out of jail."

One of them grunted. "If we know you, Arnie, you won't give it all back."

"There won't be anybody to give anything back to if you don't come along with me to the jail right now, Corey. You got to go with me on this one. And right away."

"Wait outside while we get the money, Arnie. No point in you seein' where our hidey-hole is."

Fargo straightened. The listening time was over. If Hansen came out by himself, he would have to deal with the four of them at once and there would be too much danger of the sheriff squawking out a warning to the other three.

He drew his Colt and hefted the backup revolver in his left hand.

When Sheriff Arnie Hansen stepped through the door of the shack, he was standing face to face with the Trailsman.

"Oh, shit," Hansen blurted.

"Uh huh." Fargo smiled at the sheriff.

The man might have been out of shape and bent as crooked as a hound's hind leg, but he was neither a coward nor a fool. He must have known that Fargo had been listening outside the tumbledown jacale. He saw immediately that he had only one chance, and that would be to kill the Trailsman.

Hansen gave it his best, without hesitation. His hand swept toward the butt of the revolver he wore at his belt.

Fargo shot him in the chest, and Hansen spun around, falling faceforward back inside the door to the shack.

Inside the shack there was a flurry of movement and the sound of furniture crashing over as the Calders dived for cover and grabbed for their own revolvers.

The difference in light between the brightly sunlit exterior and the shadowy inside of the place made it difficult for Fargo to see through the doorway past Hansen's body.

He saw movement and snapped a shot toward it, but he had no idea if he hit anyone or not. He ducked to the side, away from the clear line of fire through that open doorway.

A slug smashed through the flimsy wall of the jacale about chest-high, passing over Fargo's head as he crouched on the ground to the side of the door.

Fargo didn't have time for a seige. The good folk of Las Vegas were apt to take it unkindly of him to have shot down their duly elected Sheriff Arnie Hansen.

He fired into the wall in roughly the direction that shot had come from but with his aim held lower, and was rewarded by a yelp of pain and a flurry of return fire. Fargo had already moved again, shifting nearer the doorway on the assumption that the Calders would figure him to have gone the other way.

The mud plaster covering the light, pole framework of the shack burst outward as more bullets were fired blindly through the wall from inside. But Fargo had guessed correctly. The slugs came nowhere near him.

The Trailsman groaned loudly, as if he had been hit, picked up a rock, and tossed it at the base of the wall just below where the shots had come through it. The rock made a satisfyingly loud thump. He hoped the Calder boys mistook it for the sound of a body falling against the building.

"You got the son of a bitch, Wiley," someone inside said happily.

"Then finish him, Corey."

"Cover me."

Corey dived through the doorway with a shotgun in his hands. He hit the ground rolling, flattened out, and aimed the twin muzzles of the scattergun where he expected Fargo's body to be.

The instant he stopped moving, Fargo shot Corey Calder in the face. There was a brief spray of pinkish moisture in the air behind Corey's head, creating a short-lived halo effect in the sunlight.

Fargo didn't take time to watch it dissipate. He threw himself backward, falling sprawled out full-length on the ground as again the thin wall of the jacale was pocked by quick eruptions.

Two guns, Fargo noted. The shots had come too close together to have been fired by a single gun. So both Wiley and the other one, whose name Fargo hadn't heard, were still alive in there.

Fargo squirmed sideways on the hard soil, came to his knees, and crept around to the back of the place. He was taking a chance. If one or both of them made a run for freedom through the unguarded door . . .

But they didn't. Instead, they fired again.

Fargo was close to the wall. He could hear them moving just a few feet away from him.

"Keep him busy while I reload," a voice whispered.

A moment later there was the dull, hollow boom of a revolver being fired inside the shack. It was a slow, searching fire.

Fargo found a chink where the mud had flaked away from the poles. He looked through it.

A gray-and-black-striped shirt was immediately before him. The man wearing the shirt was taking his time, shooting low through the front wall where he thought Fargo might be, cocking and aiming and shooting again. His back wasn't two feet away from the back wall where Fargo now was.

Fargo drew back from the hole in the mud, put the muzzle of his Colt where his eye had just been, and tripped the trigger.

The smoke and flame from his shot spouted inside the jacale, and his bullet removed a section of the Calder boy's spine before it passed through his body and lodged against the dead man's breastbone.

Fargo spun away from the place barely ahead of another flurry of gunshots that would have ripped into his belly if he had remained where he was.

By now people for a mile around must surely be alerted to the gunfight. It would have been a bit difficult for them to avoid it.

In this immediate neighborhood, though, no one seemed to want to investigate the gunfire. The windows and shadowed doorways of the other shacks nearby were all vacant. The dark-skinned children who had been playing a few hundred yards away were no longer to be seen. Only the pigs and the chickens were left behind.

"You son of a bitch," a voice moaned from inside the jacal. "You've gone and killed my brothers. Fight me fair, you bastard, and I'll kill you."

"Come and try it," Fargo invited. He moved quickly after he spoke, expecting the last Calder to try to shoot him through the wall again. Instead, there was only the sound of someone limping across the floor inside the place.

Damned if the guy wasn't going to actually do it. He was coming outside to fight. Fargo could hardly believe it. Surely there had to be some trick involved.

Fargo slipped along the outside of the jacale to the front of the place and peered around the corner.

There he was, by damn. A mean-looking little bastard, his hair a wild tangle and his eyes even wilder. He looked damn near demented. Blood was soaking his right thigh.

Incredibly, his revolver was holstered and he was holding his hands at waist level, fingers spread and slightly hooked, ready for a fast draw.

He saw Fargo but didn't go for the gun.

"Step out where I can see you, you son of a bitch. I can take you or any man. One on one, mister. *Mano a mano*. I'll put a bullet between your eyes so fast . . ."

What the hell kind of schoolyard game was this asshole trying to play? Did he think killing was something that was supposed to be done fair and square now? After he'd howdied and then shot down those poor folks in the wagon back in Texas and stole and raped their daughter?

But then maybe it was all right for him to take advantage of others, but now that he wanted a fair fight, Fargo was supposed to holster his Colt and give Calder what he wanted. Maybe that was it.

"I'm waiting, Fargo," Calder said in a tight, emotion-choked voice. "You an' me, Fargo. *Mano a mano*."

My, oh, my, he sure had been listening to fairy tales.

Off in the direction of town there were some loud shouts. A few moments more and the people of Las Vegas would be in sight.

Fargo shrugged and shot Wiley Calder in the stomach, raised the other Colt in his left hand, and shot him again as he dropped.

Calder looked surprised . . . and disappointed.

By the time he hit the ground, he also looked dead.

Fargo turned and slipped into the low brush behind the raggedy collection of jacales, working his way wide around the town to come back into it from another direction. As soon as he was clear of the immediate vicinity, he dropped his Colt into his holster, assumed an air of innocence, and sauntered along whistling. Gunshots? What gunshots? He'd just been out for a stroll.

12

The girl nuzzled Fargo's shoulder, dropped her head a bit lower, and lipped the sensitive flesh at the side of his armpit. He felt a stir of interest, the kind that she could see just as easily as he could feel, and she laughed as she reached down to cup his balls in her palm. She squeezed gently.

"I'm game if you are," he told her.

"Good." She trailed the tip of her tongue across his chest, twirled it around his right nipple, and let it rove lower as she continued to fondle him. "Seconds are on the house, honey."

"I'm flattered," he said. He meant it. This was a business girl, and time was money. But she seemed to be enjoying his company after the unwashed teamsters and underpaid soldiers she was accustomed to receiving.

She laughed and let her tongue find its way steadily lower.

Fargo groaned and closed his eyes. She called herself FiFi, which was damned improbable, but he certainly had no complaints about her performance. Oh, my, no.

He groaned again and raised his hips to her, but FiFi

retreated with a giggle, giving him the sensation of her tongue tip but nothing more.

"Damn you," he said, but he wasn't really complaining.

FiFi laughed again, then relented. She ducked her head, engulfing him with warm heat. Deep. Deeper. Deepest. She took all of him into herself, still cupping his balls in her warm palms.

One fingernail trolled slowly over the exquisitely tender flesh between his balls and asshole. The combination of sensations was almost too much to contain, and he had to work at not spurting into her.

She released him, letting go of his cods and allowing his shaft to slide out from between her artificially red lips. "Nice?"

"Nice," he conceded in a husky croak.

She smiled at him, then moved up beside him and lay on her back, her thighs parted. "Is this all right or do you want me to finish you that way?"

"This is fine," he assured her. "Just fine."

He rolled onto his side and let his palm cover her right breast. She was built big but not at all flabby. Her nipple was hard against his palm.

FiFi smiled at him again, and he covered her. She reached between their bodies, squeezed his shaft briefly, and then guided him into her, raising her legs and canting her hips so he could slide deep inside her.

FiFi sighed at the feel of it, the sound coming at the exact same moment that Fargo sighed. He looked at her and they both laughed.

She gave him a brief, hard hug, then whispered, "Raise up. Just a bit. There. Now hold real still and let me do the work for the both of us. Yeah. Like that." She sighed again.

She moved slowly at first, raising her hips to spear his shaft deep inside her, then falling away, moving with long, sure strokes. Gradually, as her breathing quickened, the strokes became shorter and quicker, increasing tempo until she was bucking and sweating beneath him.

She began to make soft little mewling, snorting sounds of pleasure and effort, grunting and straining and driving her belly against his, impaling herself, trembling and shuddering.

Fargo felt the gather and rush of pressure deep inside his balls, felt it build and build until it could build no more, until the pleasure of it just had to find an outlet.

The outlet was there.

He grunted and spewed hot, sticky fluid deep inside her as FiFi shuddered in a quick, fluttering series of tiny convulsions, grasping him with arms and legs and lips. And most of all with hard, abrupt contractions of her sex around the base of his shaft.

"Damn," she whispered.

It wasn't a complaint, though. She sounded pleased. Satisfied. She tugged him down onto her, accepting his weight onto herself, and hugged him again.

"Nice?" she asked.

"Nice," Fargo agreed. He sighed and closed his eyes. He was completely relaxed for the first time in a very long while.

Later, he went down the stairs to the crowded saloon floor. He felt drained and loose. Pretty good, actually.

Off to the right there were a bunch of men, most of them in uniform, trying their luck at a wheel of fortune. Some others were crowded around a blackjack table.

Fargo turned left at the bottom of the stairs and joined the men who were bellied up to the bar.

The men there were already loud and were tossing the drinks down hard and heavy. It didn't take Fargo long to figure out what the main topic of conversation for the evening was going to be.

"The poor son of a bitch."

"The man's a hero, that's what he is. Was. He was a fuckin' hero."

Another fellow shook his head sadly and said, "His own kinfolk, too. Poor ol' Arnie. Had to go an' try to bring in his own kin."

"What's this all about?" Fargo asked.

The drinkers were pleased to explain it to him.

Their local law had been killed this afternoon, foully murdered by his own nephews.

"Do tell," Fargo said in wonder.

The local men told.

The way the good folk of Las Vegas reconstructed it, the Calder boys—they'd been away for the past several months with no one at all minding that they were gone—came home with trouble behind them. Sheriff Hansen had found out what they'd been up to. He went down to their place to arrest them, even if they were his own sister's boys.

The poor man—and what a good man he'd been, the locals said sadly—was doing his duty to the very last. He tried to bring those boys in, but they went and shot him down. But not before he managed to put lead into all three of those no-account boys.

Imagine that, someone asked of the stranger who was setting them up to a round of beers. Good old Arnie managed to get lead into all three of those boys before they put him down.

Fargo was thoroughly impressed by the abilities of the lamented, late sheriff. He said so loudly and often, and encouraged the local boys to tell him more while he set them up to another round. They were happy to oblige.

How they'd managed to work this all out with Arnie Hansen lying dead with his revolver unfired, well, that was something the locals had been able to work out to their own satisfaction. Fargo figured he didn't need to get picky about the details so long as they were happy with the story they'd concocted.

He smiled a little as he drained his mug and reached for the platter of free lunch cold cuts.

Obviously no one here had any notion of what had really happened at that miserable little shack.

The Trailsman damn sure intended to tell them no different.

He thought about it for a moment. There would be no need for fancy lies now. Come late night, he could slide back down there and hunt up the loot that belonged to Harry Burton's bank. No sense confusing things by mentioning that to anyone in Las Vegas, and no harm done by letting things stand as the people here believed them to be. Fargo could find the money and carry it back to San Antonio as he had promised Burton he would.

And along about that time of night there should be no problem filching the Ovaro out of that pen to carry him and the money back to San Antonio. Any formal requests that the pinto be turned over to him would just raise questions and cloud an already neat solution to the problems Fargo had expected to have.

He smiled and ordered another round for himself and his new friends. He doubted that Burton would mind him spending that expense money on some of the good people of Las Vegas.

He doubted that the banker would object to that at all.

"Have another, boys," Fargo offered. He grinned. "On me."

LOOKING FORWARD!
The following is the opening
section from the next novel in the exciting
Trailsman series from Signet:

**THE TRAILSMAN #63
STAGECOACH TO HELL**

*1860, the Montana-Idaho border.
The white man gave the land names,
Lost Trail Pass, Trapper Peak, Pioneer Mountain.
The Crow simply called the land . . . ours.*

He hadn't expected company.

And he certainly hadn't expected to be shot at naked in a pond.

But that was exactly what was happening as two more bullets grazed his ear. Fargo dived underwater as he flung another glance at the two horsemen at the edge of the small, spring-fed pond. They both fired again, the shots muffled sounds underwater as the Trailsman swam deeper. He leveled off, struck out, and surfaced at the opposite edge. He shook water from his eyes and saw the two horsemen start to race around the pond toward him. He swore softly. His clothes and gun were where he had neatly placed them on the far bank. The two riders would be at him in moments. He lifted himself, dived underwater again, glimpsing the tiny spirals of spray where two bullets slammed into the water only inches from him.

He stayed underwater until he ran out of air and surfaced in the center of the pond. The two men had halted at opposite sides of the small pond and a pair of shots bracketed him instantly. He sank again as he cursed inwardly. He couldn't keep surfacing without his luck running out, he realized as he made a half-circle underwater. They wanted him dead. He'd have to let them think they got what they wanted, and he struck out hard. He surfaced at full stroke, arms and legs flailing as he appeared to be trying to reach the far edge of the pond. He sent up sprays and splashes of water as he swam with more haste and fury than skill, and the flurry of shots sounded at once. He heard three bullets slap the water as he swam and he let out a yell of pain, throwing one arm up in the air. He filled his lungs with air as he flipped over in the water.

"We got him," Fargo heard one of the men shout before he let himself sink. He stayed underwater as long as he could, and when his chest grew tight and he felt the sharp, burning pain of lungs about to explode, he let himself go to the surface. He kept his naked body facedown as he surfaced, but managed to draw in a gasp of air out of one corner of his mouth. He lay floating inertly, legs still, face submerged, a naked, floating corpse.

"I told you we got him," he heard the rider shout.

Fargo stayed motionless in the water and heard one of the horses start to trot, rein up, halt for a moment, then go on. He listened, let the sound of both horses grow dim as the two riders cantered away. He lifted his head enough to draw in another mouthful of air and turned onto his side only when the sound of hoofbeats died away completely.

"Bastards," he swore as he swam to the edge of the pond where he'd left his clothes. He swore again as he saw that they'd taken his gun and the calf-holster with the slender, double-edged throwing knife inside it. He walked to the Ovaro where the horse rested a few yards from the pond, took a towel from his saddlebag, and dried off before pulling on clothes. He swung onto the Ovaro, his eyes on the tracks left by the two horsemen. They had gone north, and he followed, a furrow clinging to his brow.

It had all happened so quickly, so completely unexpectedly, and with no reason. But there was a reason, he knew. There was always a reason, even for the seemingly senseless. He had come upon the little spring-fed pond nestled in the hills, and it had seemed the perfect spot for a cool and cleansing dip after two days of trail riding. He'd waited, scanned the surrounding terrain for signs of Crow or perhaps passing Nez Percé or Mandan. But mostly he watched for Crow. They had been growing increasingly less tolerant of intruders on the land they looked upon as theirs. But there'd been nothing but a pair of mule deer and a pronghorn, and he'd happily shed clothes and plunged into the cold, clear water.

He'd only been in the pond for a few minutes when the two horsemen appeared, riding full out. They came charging out of the hawthorns at the east side of the pond, saw him in the water as he saw them, a case of mutual surprise. But they had instantly unholstered six-guns and began throwing lead at him. He had dived, his only recourse to prevent being shot full of holes.

Fargo felt the furrow dig deeper into his brow as he followed the hoofprints. The two men had reacted at once when they saw him looking at them. Whatever their reasons, it was all important to them that he not be around to tell anyone he'd seen them. Were they running to something or from something? His mouth tightened into a thin line. What mattered more was that they were so ready and willing to kill him just for seeing them. Anger at the thought spiraled inside him as he followed the tracks down into a narrow dip of land.

He saw both horses shorten fore and rear hoofprints. They had slowed as they entered a woodland of white fir, and Fargo took the Ovaro into the woods, stayed on the trail of hoofprints, and reined to a halt when he heard voices. He swung silently from the saddle and moved forward on foot, finally left the Ovaro with the reins dropped across a long branch, and crept on alone.

The two men came into sight, halted beside a stream. Both were out of the saddle, kneeling alongside the stream as they refilled canteens and the horses drank. Fargo took in the two figures, both ordinary, nondescript types, both medium height, one with the trace of a blond mustache, the other with a dark stubble along his chin. Fargo saw his Colt, gunbelt, and calf holster hanging from the saddlehorn of one horse and returned his eyes to the two men.

The Trailsman swore silently. There was no way he could reach them without being shot full of lead by one or the other. His eyes narrowed as he glanced back along the trail through the firs. The two men had set a fairly straight line, and he decided to bank on their continuing on straight when they crossed the stream. He pushed himself to his feet and retreated a half-dozen yards, moved on steps silent as a cougar's pads. He made a wide circle, leapt across the stream when he came to it again, and doubled back down along the far side. The two men were still resting their horses, their voices muffled through the woods.

Fargo halted beside a full, thick-limbed fir and began to pull himself up into the tree. He halted astride a low branch that bore enough foliage to conceal and enough knobby places to grip. He stretched his long legs out along the branch and waited.

He had to take out one with a single, quick, ruthless move and make the other one come to him. They hadn't thought twice about trying to kill him in the pond. He'd return the favor, Fargo commented silently, his lake-blue eyes cold as ice floes. He pushed aside idle thoughts as his wild-creature hearing picked up the sounds of a horse stepping into the stream to cross to the other bank. The two riders came into view a few minutes after, and Fargo's eyes followed the two men as they approached through the woods below. The one with the dark stubble rode closest to the tree, Fargo noted, his horse a few steps behind the other. They were almost passing beneath him and Fargo drew his legs forward on the branch, tensed powerful shoulder muscles and steel-spring thighs. He watched the two men come almost under the tree, counted off ten seconds more, and lifted himself up on the branch. He sprang as the mountain lion springs, a long, sweeping arc, every muscle taut, every fiber of his being aimed at the target, a missile of concentrated power.

Fargo slammed into the nearest rider with awesome fury, wrapped one arm around the man's neck as he swept the figure off the horse. He twisted as he fell, landed half atop the man, and he heard the sharp cracking sound of neck vertebrae snapping. He released his grip on the already limp figure and rolled sideways into a clump of bittersweet, stayed low, and saw the second man wheeling his horse around, six-gun in hand. But the rider was still recovering from his surprise, his gun raised but not aimed.

Fargo rolled again inside the bittersweet, the sound drawing two shots at once, both too fast and too high. He let himself roll again, came against the base of a big fir. A third shot slammed into the tree with a shower of wood chips.

Fargo twisted his big frame to scurry around to the

other side of the tree, and the man fired again. The Trailsman's lips edged a grim smile. The man continued to shoot too quickly from a poor angle. Fargo drew up on one knee on the other side of the tree, glanced to his rear, and spotted the line of thick sweet fern. He waited, heard the rider send his horse charging forward. When he saw the horse's snout come into sight, he flung himself backward into the sweet fern, stayed low in the thick brush as the shot whistled over his head. He pushed forward, peered back through the brush, and saw the man racing toward him, his face an angry half-snarl. The man pulled his horse up sharply as Fargo rolled to his left, then back to his right, fired again, and the shot was wide of its mark.

"Six," Fargo spit out as he leapt to his feet and charged out of the brush into the open. The man fired again and cursed as he heard only the click of an empty chamber.

"Bastard," the rider snarled, and spurred his horse forward at the big man that charged toward him.

Fargo let the horse race at him, swerved with only an inch of space left, and felt the powerful shoulders and forequarters brush past him. But he was reaching up, closed his arms around the man's leg as the horse raced by. With a curse and a shout, the rider came out of the saddle, Fargo hanging on to his leg with both arms. The man hit the ground on his back, Fargo falling with him to land half across his chest. He twisted away as the man swung the empty six-gun in a short arc, rolled aside, and leapt to his feet. He came in, avoided a second swing of the gun barrel as the man used the gun as a short club.

Fargo lashed out with a left, purposely short, and the man came in over it with the gun raised, brought the weapon down in a short, chopping motion. Fargo pulled away from the blow, crossed a looping right that caught the man high on the cheekbone with enough force to make him stagger back. Fargo's long-armed left shot out, cracked against the man's jaw, and the figure went backward, stumbled, fell to one knee.

Fargo stepped forward, lashed out with a long, low, sweeping left hook, but the man surprised him. He came in, instead of trying to pull back, wrapped both arms around Fargo's legs, and yanked. Fargo felt himself go down hard on his back, the man's arms still gripping his legs. He yanked back on his right leg, and the man let go, tried to dive forward on top of him. Fargo brought his leg up, and his knee caught the man in the chest and the figure fell to one side. Fargo started to push to his feet, but the man flung himself sideways, crashed into him at the ankles, and Fargo felt his feet go out from under him.

He pitched forward, tried to twist his body to the side, and failed. His right knee came down with all his weight behind it full on the man's throat, and he heard the gasped, gurgled sound that erupted along with a small gusher of red. Fargo let himself go forward, across the man's body, rolled to his feet, and watched the figure twitch convulsively as the stream of red grew stronger. He grimaced, cursing silently. Neither of the two would be answering any questions. When the figure gave a last, shuddered twitch and lay still, Fargo stepped around it to the horse, retrieved his gun belt and Colt and the calf-holster and knife. He walked slowly back through the woods, crossed the small stream to where he'd left the Ovaro, and climbed into the saddle.

He retraced his steps back to the pond, not hurrying, a frown creasing his brow. Curiosity more than anything else made him continue east as he picked up the trail where the two riders had come upon him in the pond. They'd been riding hard all the way, he saw from the prints that dug deeply into the ground, and he followed the clear, fresh trail down a long slope of wooded terrain. As the ground leveled off and the woods thinned out, he saw a road ahead appear, a bend almost directly in front of him. He reached it and halted, his eyes scanning the ground. The two riders had left the road at the bend and struck out north, where they'd eventually come upon him in the pond.

The bend turned out to be a long, slow curve, and it wasn't till he reached the other end of it that he saw the stagecoach halted in the middle of the road. A small knot of figures clustered around the outside of the coach, and as he rode closer, he saw that the two lead horses of what had been a four-horse team were missing. The front ends of the harness shafts were dipped low and two sets of breast collars, belly bands, and check reins lay on the ground. Fargo saw a man step forward and wave at him as he drew up to the stage, and he let his glance sweep all the figures standing by. He saw two men, three women, an old lady, and a little boy he guessed to be about seven years old.

"We're sure glad to see you, mister," the man said in a smooth voice, and Fargo took in a gray suit, a gray stetson, and a light-blue four-in-hand with a pearl stickpin. The man had a clean-shaven face made round by food, not by structure. "We've got troubles." The man nodded toward the stage.

Fargo saw with one quick glance that it was no heavy Concord, but a Brewster converted roadcoach, the driver's seat detached from the main body of the passenger compartment and an extra rear seat built high at the rear. Not so durable or heavy as the rugged Concords used by most stage lines across the West, the Brewster roadcoach had a touch more elegance of line, could hold more passengers, and take a smaller team.

"I'm Cyrus Holman," the man said, and Fargo nodded as his eyes went to the others.

"Marge O'Day," a woman said, and stepped forward.

Fargo took in a woman about thirty to thirty-five, big busts under a gray cotton dress, a little on the heavy side all over, a broad face under thick, curly blond hair that had been tinkered with to make it blonder, a face that had seen everything and could still laugh.

A man with a woman clinging to his arm moved away from alongside the coach, gray-haired, well-dressed, a tension in his face that made him seem more than the sixty-odd years he carried. The woman was half his age, Fargo saw, attractive, with a thin, long nose, dark-brown hair pulled back in a knot, and dark-blue eyes that mocked the way she clung to his arm.

"Delwin Ferris," the man said with a trace of authoritativeness. "My secretary and traveling compaion, Myrna Sayres." The woman returned Fargo's nod with a smile of cool interest. "We'd be most obliged for any help you can give us, mister." Ferris managed to make the statement sound like an order.

Fargo's glance moved to the little old lady, and he saw a small frame, not much over five feet, two inches, snapping blue eyes under a bright-blue bonnet, steel-gray hair, and a thin, sharp face. "Pauline Beal, young feller," she said in a voice that matched the snapping blue eyes.

Fargo kept the smile inside himself as he turned his gaze on the young woman and the boy. He saw dark-blond hair that hung loosely down to her shoulders, a very pretty, fine-featured face with high cheekbones and lips that would be soft and full but for the tight way she held her mouth. But it was her eyes that held him, early-morning eyes, a dusky, cloudy blue.

"I'm Charity Foster," she said as he took in a slender

figure with modestly full breasts under a square-necked dress. "This is Mitchell Blake," she said, introducing the little boy. "I'm Mitchell's governess." Fargo allowed a nod as he swung from the Ovaro and stepped to the stagecoach with Cyrus Holman beside him.

"Looks as though you lost half your team," Fargo commented.

"Lost isn't the word," Holman bristled. "They were taken, stolen, made off with right out of the harness."

Fargo's eyes narrowed. "Two men?" he asked.

"Why, yes." Holman frowned. "You see them?"

"I think so," Fargo answered. "Let me guess. They hailed you and you stopped and they took two of your horses at gunpoint, right?"

"Not exactly," Holman said. "They didn't hail us. They were our driver and shotgun rider. They just pulled to a halt, made everybody get out, and held a gun to us while they unhitched the horses. Then they rode off and left us here."

"Just like that? No talk? No robbing you? Nothing else?" Fargo frowned.

"Not a damn thing. They just took the horses and hightailed it," the man said.

Fargo's frown stayed as thoughts tumbled through his mind. "Something's wrong. Something doesn't smell right," he muttered.

"Meaning what?" Holman asked.

"I saw your two men. They tried to kill me for it," Fargo said. "That doesn't add up. They stole two horses and abandoned you. That's not enough reason for all the trouble they went to to try to kill me for seeing them. What else were they running from?"

"Search me," Holman said. "All I know is what they did to us."

"Not enough. They were riding too hard, killing too quick. Something stinks," Fargo growled. He slowly scanned the others as they watched him, saw apprehension, uncertainty, and tightness in their faces. All except Pauline Beal. In the little old lady's face he saw only irritation and impatience. His gaze lifted, moved beyond the knot of figures and the stagecoach. He'd caught the movement in the trees lining the slope, watched, and saw the leaves move again in a steady procession that meant only one thing. He kept his eyes at the top of the slope as the others followed his gaze, and he heard their quick gasps as the shapes moved out of the foliage. Three riders first, then three more followed by another cluster and still another until Fargo counted fourteen near-naked, bronzed bodies glistening in the sun.

Delwin Ferris broke the silence. "By God, there's the answer. Those two rotten cowards must have spotted the Crow and decided to run for it and save their own necks at our expense."

"Yes, that's it," Holman agreed.

Fargo, his eyes on the slope, heard Marge O'Day's voice cut in, a trace of grim amusement in it. "The big man doesn't agree," she said.

Fargo turned to her and allowed a slow smile. "Give the lady a cigar," he said. "And the name's Fargo, Skye Fargo."

"Of course, that's the explanation," Delwin Ferris insisted.

"If they were just running to save their necks, why'd they take so much time trying to kill me?" Fargo said. "There's no law against being a coward and a bastard. Something still stinks." His eyes went back to the slope and he heard the bitter edge in his voice. "But it looks as though I'm not going to be finding out what," he muttered as he peered up at the bronzed riders.

By the year 2000, 2 out of 3 Americans could be illiterate.

JllG

It's true.

Today, 75 million adults...about one American in three, can't read adequately. And by the year 2000, U.S. News & World Report envisions an America with a literacy rate of only 30%.

Before that America comes to be, you can stop it...by joining the fight against illiteracy today.

Call the Coalition for Literacy at toll-free **1-800-228-8813** and volunteer.

Volunteer Against Illiteracy. The only degree you need is a degree of caring.